THE LUMBERJANES BEASTiary

THE LUMBERJANES BEASTiary

THE MOST AMAZING GUIDE
TO ALL THE COOLEST CREATURES
YOU'VE EVER HEARD OF
AND A FEW YOU HAVEN'T

By

APRIL, JO, MAL, MOLLY, RIPLEY, AND BARNEY
(with some help from
Mariko Tamaki and Brooklyn Allen)

BASED ON THE LUMBERJANES COMICS
Created by Shannon Watters, Grace Ellis,
Noelle Stevenson & Brooklyn Allen

AMULET BOOKS
NEW YORK

Library of Congress Cataloging-in-Publication Data
Names: Tamaki, Mariko, author. | Allen, Brooklyn A., illustrator.
Title: The Lumberjanes BEASTiary : the most amazing guide to all the coolest creatures you've ever heard of and a few you haven't / by April, Jo, Mal, Molly, Ripley, and Barney (with some help from Mariko Tamaki and Brooklyn Allen).
Description: New York: Amulet Books, 2020. | Series: Lumberjanes | "Based on the Lumberjanes Comics created by Shannon Watters, Grace Ellis, Noelle Stevenson & Brooklyn Allen." | Summary: "Over the years, there have been countless magical creatures spotted at Miss Qiunzella Thiskwin Penniquiqul Thistle Crumpet's Camp for Hardcore Lady Types: mermaids, moon mice, griffins, Cloudies—you name it, the campers have seen it! But there's only one group of Lumberjanes equipped to catalog all the strange happenings at the camp: Roanoke cabin. Jo, April, Molly, Mal, Ripley, and Barney are working to earn their BEAST trophy, which is an epic project to collect all the knowledge they have about these magical creatures. Each camper will contribute their own chapters to compile an epic magical bestiary for all fans of the novels and the hit graphic novels" —Provided by publisher.
Identifiers: LCCN 2019033760 (print) | LCCN 2019033761 (ebook) | ISBN 9781419736445 (hardcover) | ISBN 9781683355618 (ebook)
Classification: LCC PZ7.T1587 Ls 2020 (print) | LCC PZ7.T1587 (ebook) | DDC [Fic]—dc23
LC record available at https://lccn.loc.gov/2019033760
LC ebook record available at https://lccn.loc.gov/2019033761

Text and illustrations copyright © 2020 BOOM! Studios
Book design by Marcie Lawrence
Coloring by Maarta Laiho
Badges designed by Brooklyn Allen, Kate Leth, and Kelsey Dieterich

Printed and bound in China
10 9 8 7 6 5 4 3 2 1

ABRAMS The Art of Books
195 Broadway, New York, NY 10007
abramsbooks.com

FOR THE
BEAST PARTNER EVER,
HEATHER. WITH LOVE,

—M.T.

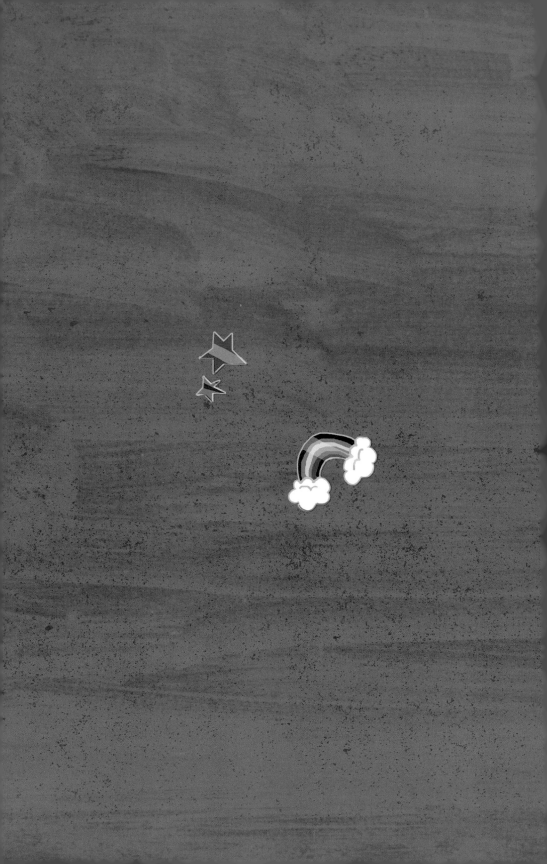

BEAST

The BEAST, or Best Everything Amazing Study Trophy, is the pinnacle of Lumberjane achievement in the area of observation and research. It is a comprehensive creature research project, a veritable, but not literal, A to Z of the wondrous world of living, breathing creatures that scouts encounter.

To receive this honor, scouts must compile and present a cross section of material that demonstrates their curiosity and ability to interact with and learn more about the world around them.

Previous BEAST trophy recipients include:

Lady Dana Deveroe Anastasia Mistytoe

Brienne Bristle "Beastly" Bonnaroo

Katy Canelope "Creature" Canasta

Frances "Fuzzy" Furnower

Rosie

Scouts are encouraged to find new, creative ways to interact with the creatures they study and to present the results of their research.

All creature contact must be mindful of the creatures and their environment and approved by supervisors before being pursued by scouts.

This research will be presented to the Lumberjanes council for review (please allow at least one week for processing).

Good luck, scouts!

Honored Members of the Lumberjane Council,

My name is Jen: Lumberjane counselor, astronomer, constant worrier.

I have had the privilege of being the counselor for Roanoke cabin, charged with the care of five bright scouts: April, Ripley, Jo, Mal, and Molly.

I am submitting these scouts, with the addition of Barney of Zodiac cabin, for the honor of the BEAST (Best Everything Amazing Study Trophy), the highest achievement in Lumber-know-how a scout can achieve.

When the scouts of Roanoke approached me with the proposition to do the BEAST and asked me to supervise along with Camp Director Rosie, I noted that this award is one often bestowed upon scouts with years' more experience than the scouts of Roanoke cabin.

I also noted that April, Ripley, Jo, Mal, Molly, and Barney are exceptional scouts, and the BEAST would be a perfect challenge for them. Because, like all good scouts, they love a challenge.

There are few scouts as dedicated and never-in-the-place-they-said-they-would-be as these six. From the time the sun peeks over the horizon to the second the moon blooms in the sky, and sometimes even much later than that, the scouts of Roanoke can be found (or not) being the best scouts they can be. In the time they have been in my charge, I have been constantly amazed, and often terrified, by their adventurous spirits and by their desire to find new, incredibly dangerous things to do.

In addition to seeking out activities that put them in peril, the scouts of Roanoke have always been voracious learners. Avid bookworms, daylight and late-night readers, they are always asking questions, wanting to understand more about the world around them. All of them have achieved their Book and See Library pins and their ReSearch Party, I Saw the Signs, Living the Plant Life, See You a Well-Rounded, Better Safety Than Sorry, Right on Track, Anthropolo-ME badges, among many more. I think it is possible that April has recently run out of room on her three badge sashes.

As part of their prep for the BEAST, they have climbed many a mountain, crossed several rivers, scaled at least a dozen treetops, and gotten into some heady conversations with many a Greek deity. They have learned about moons and meditation, breakfast habits, and new languages. And they have put it all into this collected work.

I am so delighted to be submitting these scouts for this achievement because of how they have inspired me and the other scouts at Miss Qiunzella Thiskwin Penniquiqul Thistle Crumpet's Camp for Hardcore Lady Types. I learn something new every day for knowing these scouts, which makes it worth the stress.

I think.

And so, without further ado, I present their efforts here for your consideration.

JEN

WHY THE BEAST?
WHY NOT?

A Letter of Introduction

from Roanoke Cabin

To the esteemed members of the Council,

HELLO!

We are April, Jo, Mal, Molly, Ripley, and Barney, and we want to know E-V-E-R-Y-T-H-I-N-G.

Which is to say, we want to know as much about as many things as we can possibly know. We want to know not just many things, or a lot of things, or several things, but SO MANY THINGS about SO MANY SUBJECTS.

Every time we think we've hit the edge of what we can learn about, we part the trees and there's just so much more.

And that is awesome.

The world is an amazing place with all these amazing things in it, and every minute we spend not learning about all that stuff is just . . . kind of a waste.

Every second we spend not learning about something is like saying something in the universe isn't worth learning about.

And that could never be true.

That's why being a Lumberjane is the perfect thing.

Being a Lumberjane is about taking advantage of every single second.

Being a Lumberjane is especially amazing because being a Lumberjane means always wanting to know more.

More and more, that's what we see when we read the Lumberjanes Pledge:

I solemnly swear to do my best

Every day, and in all that I do,[1]

To be brave and strong,

To be truthful and compassionate,

To be interesting and interested,[2]

To pay attention and question[3]

The world around me,[4]

To think of others first,

To always help and protect my friends,

~~To pledge a prayer to God~~

And to make the world a better place[5]

For Lumberjane scouts

And for everyone else.

THEN THERE'S A LINE ABOUT GOD, OR WHATEVER

Being a Lumberjane is about being the best Lumberjane you can be, and part of being the best Lumberjane you can be is connecting with things outside of yourself. By looking at it, writing down the stuff you see, and eventually conducting serious interview-type research.

We did this project with our whole cabin, because Lumberjanes work best when we work together. And we included our friend Barney, who is technically a part of Zodiac cabin, but really these borders are subjective and multifunctional, and Barney is supersmart when it comes to anthropological and biological study. Plus, no one knows more about safety than Barney.

---

1   Using every second of every day
2   To learn
3   And observe
4   All the stuff.
5   What better way to make the world a better place than by understanding more about it?

We interviewed mermaids, learned camp games from Cyclopses, and got some solid hair-care tips from yeti, plus we uncovered what Bearwoman eats for breakfast. And that's just the start.

Each section of this paper was prepared by a member of this team, following a general theme:

April: Literary Creatures

Jo: Flying Creatures

Mal: Creative Creatures

Molly: Greek Creatures

Barney: Creatures to Watch Out For

Ripley: Cute and Curious Creatures

In addition to our individual observations, we have all also notated one another's research, because, as Ripley says, footnotes and sidebars are like sprinkles, they make everything better.

Thank you for your consideration in the matter of this BEAST. We hope you enjoy reading this as much as we enjoyed writing it.

Signed,

April Mal Molly
Jo Ripley
and
Barney

MIGHTY APRIL!

MEET APIL!

☆ ☆ ☆

NUMBER OF BADGES: 96

FAVORITE BADGES: Pungeon Master,
Do the Write Thing

LAST BOOK READ: *The Old Mermaid
and the Sea*

FAVORITE SONG: "Let the Sunshine In"

FAVORITE CREATURE: Mermaids

SPECIALTIES: Adventure, leadership, mountain
climbing, enthusiasm, puns,
scrapbooking, enthusiasm!

I like the crisp smell of adventure and the
shiny brightness of a cool new thing. I love
reaching new heights and then parachuting down
from those heights on the back of a strong wind.

9

CREATURES OF LITERATURE

OFF THE PAGE AND IN YOUR FACE!

by April

I have a very extensive list of favorite things. Very high up on that list are books—subcategory: books about magical beasts, subcategory: books about fairies, unicorns, mermaids, and sea monsters.

I grew up reading, a lot. When I was lonely, I knew that all I had to do was open a book and I would be transported to a world of cool.

One of the reasons I like books about magical creatures is that they open the door to imagining something other than your everyday or imagining that somewhere inside your everyday is something you couldn't imagine. Something amazing. I like books that create worlds to explore, maybe because I really really really like exploring.

It's entirely possible that I became a Lumberjane in the first place because I wanted to live out the adventures I was reading about. Holy Holly Black, was THAT a great decision!

The world of the Lumberjanes is a little like a giant adventure book, where every page is a new adventure, a new creature, a new world. In some ways, every creature I have met is a story, and each becomes part of my story (which I think is a pretty great story at this point). In other ways, they are so much more.

For me, the great gift of the BEAST is to be able to document the amazing creatures I have met in my adventures, who are really so much grander than you could fit on a page. Some of these creatures have appeared in fairy tales, some can be found in mythologies from around the world. All are amazing.

I have tried to capture their humor and their wisdom, their sweetness and their power. Each of these creatures is unique and incredible, and I am fortunate to have been able to meet them all. I will never forget them.

APRIL,
ACTUALLY
CLIMBING
EVERY
MOUNTAIN!

MERMAID THAT WAY

by April

CREATURE CATEGORY: Amazing Aquatic

DANGER LEVEL: 4

HABITAT: Bodies of water

DIET: Fish, kelp, popcorn

FAVORITE CATCHPHRASE: Water you talking about?

CREATURE PEEVES: Water pollution, water serpents, speedboats

Merfolk, or mermaids, are creatures of the sea, and they are both beautiful and complex. Mermaids have appeared in stories from ancient Greek mythology to modern Western pop culture. They are portrayed as fearful and romantic figures, known for luring sailors to their deaths and falling in love with the wrong men (see page 16 for full story of "The Little Mermaid").

Some scouts may also be familiar with merfolk from the unbelievable super-fantastic Mermaid Lemonade Stand series, which includes amazing books like *Misty and the Clam Next Door* and *Sea Average.* (If you have never read these books, you are advised to go to the library RIGHT NOW and get them and read them RIGHT NOW.)

No matter which literary genre they appear in, some elements of mermaids remain constant: They are creatures that are half person, half fish, or half fish and half person, depending on how you think about it. They generally have a fish tail and a human top half and really amazing hair. Gills optional. Mermaids dwell in bodies of water, including oceans, rivers, and lakes, and they can breathe, talk, and sing underwater.

Technically, there are multiple identities that can be referred to under the umbrella of what is often generalized as merMAIDS. There are some who like to be called merwomen and some who prefer mermen. Others prefer merfolk. It is always best to ask the MER in question how they want to be addressed before you assume calling them anything.

The best way to find out about modern merfolk is to talk to an actual mer-person, so I have included here my interview with Taylor, who I met in a lake this summer.

Roanoke first encountered real, in-the-flesh mermaids when April came upon the mermaid Taylor in a lake just outside of camp. It's actually kind of a funny story involving sea serpents, broken friendships, mer-rock bands, and April wearing a sort of ad hoc scuba suit whipped up by Jo. You could say that the story involves April saving the day . . . but it's actually a little more complicated than that. Needless to say, it did end with some solid rocking out and lots of GLITTER, which is how any good Lumber-tale should end.

Okay, here's the interview:

☆ ☆ ☆

APRIL: Hi, Taylor.

TAYLOR: Hey, April. How's it going?

APRIL: GOOD! Thanks for doing this interview.

TAYLOR: Thanks for coming into the lake. Nice scuba suit.

APRIL: Thanks! It's new. Jo made it.

TAYLOR: Cool.

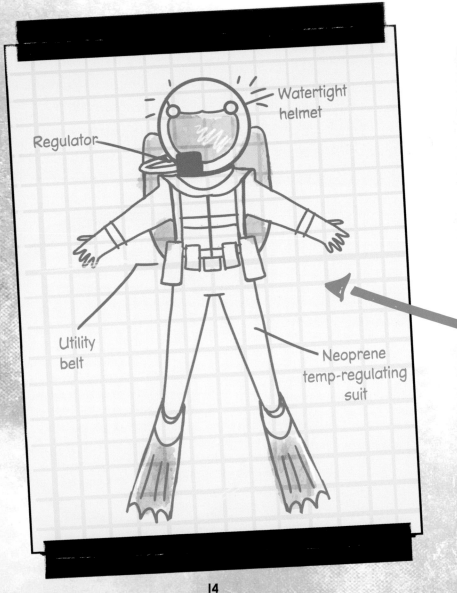

APRIL: You can breathe air and water, though, right?

TAYLOR: I can breathe air, but I don't really like to. It makes me sneezy.

APRIL: RIGHT! Questions. Okay, so, first question. Very important. Are you a fan of the Mermaid Lemonade Stand series?

TAYLOR: DUH. Obviously. I've been reading the Mermaid Lemonade Stand series since I was a GUPPY!

APRIL: AMAZING.

TAYLOR: When I was a mer-tyke I read *I Can Sea Stars*. Mera, I loved that book! Now I'm super grouper into the Mermaid Lemonade Stand crime series, *Sea Red*.

APRIL: I love *Sea Red*!

TAYLOR: You know that a mermaid writes them, right?

APRIL: NO, I DIDN'T. THAT'S SO COOL.

TAYLOR: I think she has a land name she publishes under, just for privacy's sake. Because, you know, avid fans. You don't want schools of Lemonheads banging down your door.

APRIL: What's a land name?

My guess is that the books must be written with some version of a pencil, since all ink, underwater, would bleed.

The original scuba suit and its component parts, including the air pump and regulator, date back to the early 1700s. There have been two previous versions of April's Lumber-scuba suit, both invented by me. The first was an incredibly rudimentary model with an air hose with no regulator. The second, created for night diving, was fitted with a proper demand regulator and a light. This current version is more lightweight, thanks to the help of Heddie, who is a ghost and great inventor as well. (See page 91.)

TAYLOR: It's like a pen name, a name you use for publishing, but it's a land dweller name.

APRIL: Right. That makes sense. Wait, does that mean I can have a mer-name?

TAYLOR: OH. Maybe. I don't know. I can't really give permission for all mer-kind.

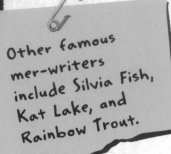

Other famous mer-writers include Silvia Fish, Kat Lake, and Rainbow Trout.

APRIL: Fair enough. That's cool that mer-people like the Mermaid Lemonade Stand series. It would be sad if it was stereotypical or, you know, misrepresenting.

TAYLOR: I heard she started writing because someone gave her a copy of "The Little Mermaid" by Hans Christian Andersen, and she was like, "I don't know who this is, but they don't know KELP about mermaids." So she started writing her OWN books.

APRIL: That's awesome. More people should do that!

1. A mermaid is happy in her underwater palace.
2. She turns fifteen and sees a prince.
3. She falls in love with the prince.
4. She ends up saving the prince from drowning (not that he knows it's her).
5. She gives up being a mermaid in order to be with the prince, which means giving up not just her TAIL but her TONGUE and her VOICE (kind of related). And she will always have foot pain.

6. She'll also lose her soul unless the prince marries her (patriarchy!).
7. Turns out the prince ends up marrying some other princess who he thinks is the girl who saved him from drowning, but it's NOT. (It's the Little Mermaid! Hello!)
8. The mermaid gets an out from her sisters (who give up their hair) that she can become a mermaid again IF she kills the prince.
9. But she doesn't.
10. And she ends up being sea foam forever.

TAYLOR: Well, we all have our inspirations.

APRIL: Oh, yeah. So what are other names you guys have for people who live on land?

TAYLOR: Mostly we call you all land dwellers, or non-mers. Or, in your case, just April.

APRIL: What's the best part of being . . . Wait what do you prefer? Mermaid or . . . ?

TAYLOR: Mergirl. For me.

APRIL: What's the best part of being a mergirl?

TAYLOR: Um. I don't know, really. My friends, all the seaweed I can eat, my tail. Fish are fun once you get to know them. All of it really. I mean, you know, I've only ever been a mergirl, so it's hard to tell.

APRIL: Is there anything particularly difficult about being a mergirl?

TAYLOR: Oh yeah. Water serpents can be kind of a pain in the coral. They swoop in and bust stuff up from time to time, and you need to be careful when they're with their young because they're super protective. But generally, if you talk to them, they chill out.

APRIL: Do you speak water serpent?

TAYLOR: Doesn't everyone?

Water serpents: Large lizard- or dragon-sized creatures found in fresh and salt water. Should be avoided at all times. They ARE a pain in the coral and sometimes big enough to eat a canoe!

APRIL: Um. Not that I know of. What else do you speak?

TAYLOR: I speak most crustacean, shark, dolphin, whale . . . I guess most fish species, except goldfish. I'm still learning anemone. They have a lot of verbs.

It is the humble opinion of this writer that the Lemonade Stand series book *The Other Little Mermaid*, about a mermaid who keeps her voice and uses it to tell off a prince for water pollution practices, is a much better story.

APRIL: So, you can talk to your anemones the way you talk to your friends?

TAYLOR: Is that an anemone pun?

APRIL: Yes, it is.

TAYLOR: Yeah. Maybe not surprisingly, sea anemones hate puns.

APRIL: Right. I'll try to remember that.

TAYLOR: Actually, of all the languages, probably the trickiest is shark.

APRIL: Because they want to eat you?

TAYLOR: Not all of them, but some of them, yeah.

APRIL: What kind of music do mermaids like?

TAYLOR: I mean, all kinds. I like punk rock, rock, ska, modern jazz, and classical. But that's just me.

APRIL: Is there a kind of music that's JUST mermaid music?

TAYLOR: There is a specific sound merfolk can produce that's only for underwater play. It's called SQUEEEEEEE. It's very loud. It sometimes summons whales. It rocks.

APRIL: SO COOL! So, what's your new band called?

TAYLOR: Right now we're called TIDAL RIOT, but that could change.

APRIL: What do you want to be when you grow up?

TAYLOR: A mergirl . . . with a bigger tail. Maybe two more guitars would be nice.

APRIL: Any other words for the scouts out there reading this?

TAYLOR: Water conservation is a thing! Save water so me and my friends will have a home in the next decade.

APRIL: Thanks, Taylor!

TAYLOR: ((SQUEEEEEE))!

APRIL: AMAZING!

DIARY OF A GROOTSLANG FAN

by April

CREATURE CATEGORY: Mystical Land Creature

DANGER LEVEL: 8

GROUCHY LEVEL: 7

HABITAT: Caves, if you can find them, which you probably won't

DIET: Whatever they want

FAVORITE CATCHPHRASE: I know.

ENJOYMENT OF PUNS: Low

CREATURE PEEVES: Radio static, visitors, people, guests

A featured creature of South African lore, there are few beasts as magnificent and, frankly, as super ancient as the Grootslang, a creature that is part elephant, part snake, and all awesome.

Grootslang are as ginormous as the most ginormous tree, like the kind that touch the sky, and gray, with long ivory tusks that may or may not be venomous (let's not find out) and big floppy ears that are not at all floppy in a cute way. Sometimes they have gems for eyes that flash like the fires of some forbidden fiery place no scout can tread on.

Originally from the continent of Africa, Grootslang have spread around the world but are notoriously difficult to find.

In addition to being incredibly powerful, Grootslang are also very fond of sparkly things, which makes them SUPER amazing. They are very protective of their sparkly things, and losing their sparkly things makes them really mad. Which is scary,

because Grootslang are super big, and they can bring down mountains with just a growl (although, admittedly, a pretty big growl).

The Grootslang in closest proximity to the Lumberjane Camp has a gem, a heart stone, embedded in its Chest. This gem was originally stolen from the Grootslang by a former Lumberjane named Abigail, who was also seeking to slay the Grootslang in order to add it to her giant stuffed animal collection. Fortunately, before she could complete her hunt, Abigail was intercepted by Roanoke cabin with the able assistance of Rosie and Jen.

This is actually probably the least scary story ever told about a Grootslang. It ends with the Grootslang getting its gem back, Abigail breaking her arm, Jen driving in an avalanche, and Barney eventually joining the Lumberjanes.

Lumberjanes in no way condone or support the stealing of gems, or stones, or ANYTHING from the stomachs, or cupboards, or suitcases, or ANYTHING of any creature great or small. NOT COOL.

Observing the Grootslang presents an obvious conundrum for those of us interested in observing incredible creatures. Grootslang, like many creatures, have a long and complicated history with people: people taking their gems, hunting them, and generally bothering them, which makes them incredibly leery of people. This particular Grootslang had declared its mountain off-limits to the Lumberjanes after a series of pretty crummy experiences (see sidebar). Fortunately, Camp Director Rosie was able to repair Grootslang relations after discovering a sapphire the size of a bowling ball that had rolled out of the Grootslang's cave. In gratitude for its return, the Grootslang agreed to participate in this study. Provided the study wasn't too annoying.

And so here is a documentation of my time with the Grootslang.

Monday

The Grootslang lives in a cave at the edge of the forest. The cave is at least a day's hike up the face of a sheer cliff (not a problem for an experienced climber). Although the entrance is small, the cave inside is very roomy, if a little gloomy. It is moderately furnished with a small table and a radio and a kettle on a fire. And a giant Grootslang bed, which is really just a lot of felled trees. There are several rocks I assumed were "chairs." They are not comfortable. Cave is chilly but not cold.

Related Badge Skill:
GET ON UP!

Arrived at sunup. Assumed this would be prime Grootslang hours. Turns out Grootslang does not care about sunup. Or sundown. Grootslang slept till noon. Woke and made us tea, because like a few other creatures we've encountered, the Grootslang likes a morning cup of loose-leaf tea (see Cloudies, page 58). Turned the radio on. Grootslang prefers talk radio, specifically weather reports, although Grootslang does not like to go out of cave. Grootslang spent the day discussing the Mongol invasions, which ended around 1405, but maybe the Grootslang is very old and doesn't know that this was a long time ago? Or maybe Grootslang just really likes history. Not sure. Grootslang did not ask me any questions, and at various points, I think, forgot I was there and was just talking to the cave. After discussing the Mongols, the Grootslang said it was time for a nap and asked me to leave. I did.

Tuesday
Grootslang slept all day.

Wednesday

Grootslang slept all day.

(Grootslang actually slept all week, so I came back on the following . . .)

Thursday

Grootslang woke with a start. Did not ask me what day it was. Then Grootslang spent the day listening to a radio show about woodworking. Grootslang is a huge fan of woodwork and spent the day talking about the history of people using wooden tools, which obviously predates the use of metal tools. I mentioned the Mesolithic practice of using metal to fashion arrowheads and other weaponry. The Grootslang was possibly pleased and possibly annoyed that I knew this. I told the Grootslang I have my May the Forge Be with You badge for metalsmithing. The Grootslang said that was not interesting and turned back to its radio.

Two hours later, the Grootslang did quiz me on the previous week's discussion. I correctly answered the Grootslang's question. The answer was the Volga River, and the Grootslang did not kick me out. I watched the Grootslang have tea. I wonder if it would be okay for me to ask the Grootslang questions if we are quizzing each other on things.

Friday

It is not okay. I brought questions for the Grootslang on the origins of government and other historical subjects. Grootslang hates being quizzed. I was asked to leave, so I did.

Saturday

Grootslang was up earlier than usual. Spent day listening to auctions on the radio and discussing the history of bartering systems with me. I told Grootslang that bartering is a good system, but it is not what most people use these days, although technically, as a Lumberjane, I barter with my fellow scouts, as we don't use cash at camp. But this is an exception. The Grootslang and I then debated the benefits of capitalism, which the Grootslang does not think is a very good system for exchange, because, I think, Grootslangs don't have money, only lots of gems. The Grootslang said capitalism is a trend. I said that might be true. The Grootslang said, "Check back with me in a century. I'm right." Notably, Grootslangs are pretty self-sufficient since all they want are the gems they have and tea. So they don't really need to barter for anything. I mentioned this to the Grootslang, and it said it was mostly interested in the subject in theory.

Sunday

Things I learned from the Grootslang today: The Grootslang was once in a barbershop quartet, enjoys lawn bowling, and is interested in taking up macramé so it can acquire some hanging plants for its cave. The Grootslang also enjoys golf, not playing golf but talking about golf and its evolution as a game that people now wear fancy clothes to play (not that the Grootslang watches TV, but the Grootslang has heard this is a thing). Overall, I would say the Grootslang enjoys general knowledge, like discussing the history of roads. I have taken to combing through the encyclopedia at night after hanging out with the Grootslang in the hopes that I might hit on some trivia the Grootslang will find interesting. Today I lucked out and was able to contribute to a conversation on herd dogs and what breeds of dogs work well as herd dogs. I made a pun, saying, "I HERD border collies are very effective." The Grootslang did not laugh, but very few people laugh at puns. The Grootslang made tea in the afternoon and made me a cup as well. Grootslangs don't really have cups, but there was a giant rock with a divot at the top that the Grootslang poured tea from its trunk into. I have never drunk anything from anyone's trunk, but I thought it would be super rude if I didn't and that this was kind of a huge deal, so I had a sip and then said I was full. The Grootslang noted that I am very small, then turned on a radio program about geese.

Monday

I went back and the Grootslang had covered the hole to its cave with giant rocks. Don't know if this is how Grootslangs say goodbye or if maybe I should have finished my tea.

Final Observations

There are many things a scout could say that are surprising about Grootslang: their size, their jewels, and their relative rareness.

Here is the thing I found most surprising: Grootslang are more like my grandma Beverly than I could have ever imagined.

1. They listen to the radio all day. (Also, where do the Grootslang get radios?)
2. They love talking about things that are not immediately practical and are subjects it would seem appropriate to talk about while wearing wool (although, Grootslang do not). These topics include: the weather, the manipulation of various materials, and history.
3. They do not like being interrupted.
4. They think they know more than me.
5. They are very old, so maybe they do.
6. They sleep A LOT.
7. I think if the Grootslang ever DID want to make money, the Grootslang could go on a television quiz show. Although, the idea of a Grootslang game show in and of itself would blow everyone's mind, probably. So maybe not.

Final conclusion: Grootslang are amazing ancient creatures who should be respected, like grandparents.

Also: I wonder if I introduced my grandmother, who also likes gems, to a Grootslang if they would get along. Possible next adventure.

GEOFF THE GRIFFIN

by April

CREATURE CATEGORY: Mythological Mixed Mammal Bird

DANGER LEVEL: 8

HABITAT: Mountainous areas

DIET: Whatever they feel like

FAVORITE CATCHPHRASE: CERRAP!

CREATURE PEEVES: Egg thieves, bad music

With the body of a lion, and the head, claws, and wings of an eagle, the griffin has often appeared in literature, symbolizing strength and nobility.

Images of griffins, or similar bird/beast creatures, can be found in ancient Iranian, Egyptian, Cretian, and Hindu art.

Griffins have made significant appearances in Greek and Roman texts, as well as a host of other mythologies. Most notable appearances include Dante's Divine Comedy and John Milton's Paradise Lost (which I am halfway through). Younger readers might recognize the Griffin from Lewis Carroll's Alice in Wonderland and J. K. Rowling's Harry Potter series.

Griffins are also referred to as gryphon and griffon.

In most stories and myths, griffins are deadly, gold, and mysterious. Generally, they exist to guard precious things and scare off unwanted guests. They pull chariots and look, and *are*, intimidating.

But of course, not all griffins are like this!

As an example, here is the story of a griffin named Geoff.

GEOFF THE GRIFFIN

SO RAD!

Geoff was not like the other griffins.

He did have the head of a bird and the body of a lion, and he had sharp claws, also called talons, so he **LOOKED** like other griffins. BUT, while the other griffins liked to pierce the air with their sharp cries and squawks, Geoff . . . liked to croon.

It is not that griffins do not like singing, they do, but they are very picky about what kind of singing and as a whole they mostly despise crooning.

And they REALLY don't like griffins that croon.

And so it was that there was only one crooning griffin in the history of crooning. Which was Geoff.

But Geoff really loved to croon. He even wrote his own jazz standard, "The Griffin from Ipanema." The only griffin jazz standard ever written.

This song was sung (crooned) at the only griffin crooning concert in the history of the griffin world, which took place this summer.

Geoff rented a stage in the forest for the concert. He rehearsed for weeks. To publicize it, Geoff printed out flyers and he passed them out to all his griffin friends. Most of the griffins didn't even read the flyer. They just looked at it and recycled it. Because griffins recycle.

The night of the concert, Geoff got ready to go onstage. Geoff figured that no one was coming. That he would be all alone, crooning to rows of empty stumps.

And then . . . he spotted someone.

That night, Geoff found out that there was only one griffin crooner in the world, but there was also one griffin crooning fan.

And he sang all night long.

And he was one of the two happiest griffins of all time.

THE END

MOLLY AND BUBBLES! BEST RACCOON AND SCOUT FRIENDS FOREVER!

MEET MOLLY!

☆ ☆ ☆

NUMBER OF BADGES: 26

FAVORITE BADGES: That's Accordion to You,
Astrono-me-me-me

LAST BOOK READ: *The Complete Book of Deities*

FAVORITE SONG: "Closer to Fine"

FAVORITE CREATURE: BUBBLES!

SPECIALTIES: Archery, music, astronomy,
Greek mythology

i guess you could say i'm a multifaceted scout in that i love a lot of different things, and i'm always finding new things to nerd out on.

A GREEK GOD BY ANY OTHER NAME

by Molly

Greek myths. They're exciting, daring, torturous and tumultuous, violent and frustrating. They're about jealousy and betrayal, victory and defeat, and I love them. For as long as I can remember, the world of Greek myths was a world in the clouds for a girl with her head in the clouds, who is me.

When I was a kid, my parents hated music (and radios, and TV, and pretty much anything that made noise), but they had a huge library in the living room, the center of which was a massive collection of Greek mythology: leather-bound books with gold lettering that took two hands to get off the shelf. Instead of Taylor Swift, I had the stories of Hera, Artemis, and Cassandra. Instead of Saturday-morning cartoons, I had the tragic tales of anyone who crossed paths with Zeus. And a lot of people did.

I will admit, actually meeting figures from Greek mythology wasn't always as awesome as a younger me might have thought. I guess that's because, when you meet them, Greek gods are gods, but they're also scouts, parents, friends, and siblings.

They get annoyed when you forget their name. They're kind of bossy sometimes (I mean, when you're used to being a GOD I guess that makes sense). They're not super great at losing at board games (they're actually HORRIBLE losers, so maybe don't play board games with the next Greek deity you run into). Sometimes they try and destroy your camp just because they find that sort of thing amusing.

What I learned from this project is that these mythological figures are dealing with both deity-level complicated things and everyday things, like overbearing parents and family pressures.

I'm glad I got to spend time with these very interesting figures. Talking to them taught me that there is always another layer to be revealed. There's the myth you know and the figure behind the myth, which can be just as complex, fascinating, and inspiring.

DON'T MESS WITH DIANE

by Molly

CREATURE CATEGORY: Greek Deity

DANGER LEVEL: 8

ANNOYED LEVEL: 9

HABITATS: Mount Olympus, Miss Qiunzella Thiskwin Penniquiqul Thistle Crumpet's Camp for Hardcore Lady Types

DIET: Vegetarian, for the moment

FAVORITE CATCHPHRASE: UGH. FINE.

CREATURE PEEVES: Rudeness, Apollo, everyone in her family

FAVORITE THING: Winning

Diane first became a scout at Miss Qiunzella Thiskwin Penniquiqul Thistle Crumpet's Camp for Hardcore Lady Types this summer and quickly became a notable, forceful part of camp life. I think having a scout who's an actual Greek deity is a tribute to the amazingness of camp, which is like a jelly bean jar full of big flavorful personalities, and also a home away from home for this Greek deity.

Diane, like many scouts, has a few names she goes by, although admittedly it's a few more than the average scout.

The Greeks referred to her as Artemis and goddess of the hunt, the wilderness, wild animals, the moon, and chastity.

Which is a sizable description and a lot of responsibility.

The Romans referred to her as Diana, a name change which they did to most of the Greek gods.

At camp, Diane prefers *Diane*, because, she says, it's just always sounded like a cooler name.

In our interview for this profile, which took place in Diane's Zodiac cabin, Diane said that learning

Other name changes:
Aphrodite became Venus.
Ares became Mars.
Apollo became . . . Apollo.
Weird.

to be a scout, rather than a deity to be worshipped, was difficult. While most scouts have to get used to sharing a cabin, Diane had to get used to not just camp life, but also to life among mortals.

"FINE, yes," Diane admitted. "So I did ALMOST turn Hes into a deer on the first day . . . accidentally. She was bugging me."

Hes explained that Diane DID turn her into a deer, but only briefly. And she added that it was rad. Because deer are rad. Hes said that if it happened again, she wouldn't be too mad, so long as Diane changed her back.

Turning people into deer is something Diane comes to pretty naturally. Notably, Diane's father, Zeus, is both the king of the gods and the god of the sky, lightning, thunder, law, order, and justice, and he once turned someone into a cow. (Probably more than once, Diane said.)

It should also be noted that Zeus can turn HIMSELF into various things, including a swan, an ant, and a bull (which is really just a very small section of the list). Generally, Zeus did this to seduce women. Which . . . I don't really understand, but that's Greek mythology for you!

One of Diane's real learning curves as a scout was dealing with what Jen calls "conflict resolution." Conflict resolution, in general, is not something Greek gods are well known for. Really, what Greek gods are known for is conflict.

Diane shrugs. "I mean, yeah, where I come from, when we get mad, we turn people into stags, we banish them, we throw a lightning bolt at them, we curse them . . . That's just how we do things, okay? Where I come from, you look at someone the wrong way, we turn you into stone. It's just way easier than talking about stuff."

The members of Roanoke cabin have found themselves in the middle of many a Greek conflict, including a fight between Diane and her brother, Apollo, which briefly resulted in Jo being turned to stone and transported to another very lonely dimension. Fortunately, with a little teamwork and puzzle solving, all was sorted, and now Diane is a part of the Lumberjane crew!

36

Diane says that while at camp, with the help of her cabinmates, including Barney, she has considered the possibility of exploring other methods for resolving conflict, like having clear boundaries and just talking to people instead of turning them into things. Diane said that this is the first time she has ever actually had friends, too, which she said is better than just having a lot of people who are afraid of you.

Related Badge Skill:
FRIENDSHIP TO THE MAX!

With that in mind, Diane provided me with a few brief dos and don'ts she would appreciate people following while she's at camp.

DIANE'S TOP 10 DOS AND DON'TS

DO call her Diane.

DON'T forget that she is ALSO Diana, goddess of the woods, children, childbirth, fertility, chastity, the moon, and wild animals. And you are not.

DO know your mythology. Greek mythology isn't just a bunch of good stories, it's the basis for many names and is referenced in almost every walk of life. Not knowing Greek mythology is very annoying to people who ARE Greek mythology.

DON'T get in a Greek god's way. Greek gods are complicated, unpredictable, and good at fighting with each other. Just about everyone who gets in the way PAYS.

DO avoid her brother, Apollo, who is super annoying, and who Diane is kind of competitive with.

DON'T ask her what it's like to be a Greek god. If you ARE a Greek god and have been one your whole life, you have nothing to compare it to, and it's a stupid question.

DO protect the Earth. As the goddess of wild animals, among many other things, the environment is an incredibly important issue for Diane. If you take care of the Earth that the animals of the world need to survive, then Diane will make sure you probably won't end up as a clump of grass.

DON'T come after her cabin, Zodiac, which is the best cabin. Or she'll turn you into a cow.

DO watch out for other Greek deities and creatures, because once you have one Greek god at camp, there's bound to be more on the way.

THE GORGONS

It's true that since Diane's arrival, Miss Qiunzella Thiskwin Penniquiqul Thistle Crumpet's Camp for Hardcore Lady Types has been visited by a host of other Greek figures of repute. One notable unexpected guest was a Gorgon, Ligo. The Gorgons, descendants of Medusa, were cursed by Athena to have snakes for hair and the added misfortune of turning everyone they look at into stone (in yet another example of why it's not a good idea to get into a fight with a Greek deity). Ligo intentionally avoided opening her eyes to prevent turning people to stone.

The unfortunate part of the Gorgon's Lumberjane story was that she got blamed for turning some campers to stone. The fortunate part was that Roanoke eventually figured out that it wasn't Ligo, AND, with Ligo's and Diane's help, helped un-stone everyone AND they learned that snakes have an incredible sense of smell, which helped Ligo navigate without her eyes!

CYCLOPS GAMES

by Molly

CREATURE CATEGORY: Mystical Land Roaming

DANGER LEVEL: 7

METALSMITHING SKILL LEVEL: 10

HABITATS: Heaven and earth, places where molten lead flows

DIET: Varies

FAVORITE CATCHPHRASE: Eye'll be the judge of that (and other eye puns)

CREATURE PEEVES: Eye patches, jokes about having one eye not made by a Cyclops

The Cyclops has what is probably my favorite feature on any creature: a large, singular eye at the center of its forehead.

From the Greek word *Kuklōps*, or "circle-eyed"

According to the Greek poet Hesiod, who was a pretty great Greek poet, Cyclopses are actual descendants of heaven and earth, aka Uranus (sky) and Gaia (earth).

So when you say something like "Where are you from?" Cyclopses are some of the few creatures that can say "Heaven" and it's not a joke.

The original Cyclopses had some of the most amazing names in Greek mythology: Brontes (Thunder), Steropes (Lightning), and Arges (Bright). They were brothers of the Titans, and they were symbolic of strength and power, the fires of the forge, and the art of blacksmithery.

Related Badge Skill:
MAY THE FORGE BE WITH YOU

The most recent visitor to Miss Qiunzella Thiskwin Penniquiqul Thistle Crumpet's Camp for Hardcore Lady Types was actually a BISON Cyclops, a unique and cuddly twist on the Cyclops family whose eye could record and project images from the past into the present. This neat trick helped save a supercool cowgirl named Emmy, the head of the Bison's Zoo Crew, a ragtag herd of creatures that included a basilisk, a hodag, and a squirrel hatched from an egg!

In addition to metalsmithing, the Cyclopses' other favorite hobby is games, specifically the kind of games that are apparently played at Cyclops parties (which are very hard to get invited to). Listed in order of preference from least to most, are the Cyclopses' favorite camp games.

1. Run and Freeze—aka Orpheus and Eurydice

In this game, one Cyclops, Orpheus, stands on one end of the field while the rest, the Eurydices, line up at the other end. To start the game, Orpheus calls out "RUN" and the Eurydices sprint toward him. Then Orpheus calls out "STOP" and spins around. Anyone Orpheus caught still running is out. The trick is to make it over the line before Orpheus spots you. The Cyclopses admit the origins of this game are sort of tragic, but feel like it's a solid way to remind people about the history of Greek tragedy while still getting in some legit cardio.

2. Horseshoes

The Cyclopses are renowned blacksmiths, known for their skill with metal and fire and for their love of playing endless games of horseshoes with the fruits of their labor. The beauty of horseshoes is that anyone with a horseshoe and a few feet of turf, sand, or clay can play. All you need is a stake (ideally one foot tall above the ground) and four horseshoes per player. Generally, the foul line, where the player tosses the shoe from, is at least thirty feet from the stake. But if you are a ten-foot-tall Cyclops, a little extra space is ideal. Shoes are tossed underhand with the goal of a "ringer," a shoe that ends up encircling the stake, or a "leaner," a shoe that lands at least six feet from the stake. The game is over when a player reaches the agreed-upon score.

3. Eye Spy

It was a surprise to hear this classic car game was a favorite of most Cyclopses. Eye Spy is a game of observation and guessing, with one player spotting an object and calling it out with the phrase "Eye spy with my giant eye something that is _____," for example, blue. Then the other player has to guess what the blue object is. Apparently, Bert "Big Eye" Cyclops and Bernie "Blinks" Cyclops have been playing a single game of Eye Spy for the past hundred years. Bernie is still looking for a green thing. He hopes to discover it sometime in the next decade.

4. Ephedrismos

It's probably not surprising that this popular Greek children's game is also popular with Cyclopses. The game is played by two Cyclopses (or people), who take turns trying to hit a stone with a rock (or whatever projectile is handy). The Cyclops who misses by the most has to carry the winner on their back with their eye covered and try to touch the rock with their foot.

As Jo discovered on a recent Greek adventure, a handy person to play this game with is a Gorgon, since Gorgons are pretty good at navigating with snakes and smell and don't use their eyes!

CASSIE'S WOODEN WONDERS

by Molly

CREATURE CATEGORY: A Lumberjane with a Greek history

DANGER LEVEL: 6

WOOD SKILLS: 8

PREDICTIVE ABILITY SKILLS: 7

HABITAT: Predictable places

DIET: Vegan

FAVORITE CATCHPHRASE: Predictive and unnerving statements

CREATURE PEEVES: Bad horoscopes, unexpected weather, splinters

Daughter of Hecuba and Priam, the last king of Troy, Princess Cassandra was a complicated character in Greek history (one of MANY, if you think about it), and her great-great-great-great-great-great-grandniece, Cassie, heir to her powers, is no different.

Cassie describes herself as having two inheritances. The first is the gift of sight, which came into play at camp when she had a brief stint writing horoscopes for the Lumberjanes newsletter (before we all decided that this was a bad idea because her spooky, spot-on predictions were freaking everyone out). The gift of sight, Cassie says, is a complicated one, sometimes disturbing and unhelpful.

Her second legacy is that of the Trojan horse. The Trojan horse was a giant wooden horse sent by the Greeks to Cassie's great-great-great-great-great-great-great-aunt Cassandra's home, Troy, where it was presented as a gift. But hiding inside this gift (which wasn't really a gift) was an army of Greek soldiers. Once the wooden horse was rolled through the gate, the soldiers spilled out and destroyed Troy. Tragically, Cassandra was the only one who saw the horse for what it was. No one believed her.

Cassie has opted to turn this dark symbol in her family's history into something positive and functional. After developing an interest

The original Cassandra story took a definite wrong turn when she caught the attention of Apollo, who promised her the power of prophecy if she did what he wanted. She didn't, so Apollo gave her the power of prophecy but threw in the added glitch that no one would believe what she said. This is actually a pretty horrible story, because why can't Cassandra just make her own choices? I didn't say this to Cassie, but I think Apollo is a jerk.

in architecture and woodworking, she set to task on a project that has become something of an obsession: making massive, wooden, livable structures that come in the shape of unexpected objects.

Related Badge Skill:
BECAUSE I HAVE A HAMMER

At a recent camp exhibit, she displayed a series of her most recent works. All of these structures are on wheels and can be fitted with outboard motors or dragged behind a vehicle as a trailer. All will fit a small army of scouts.

The Wooden Bunny

Inspired by the rabbits of the plains, the creatures that hear danger before anyone else, these wooden rabbits are perfect for quick trips to the farmers market and anywhere else you need to hop to! Made from maple, these are incredibly sturdy. Fits a herd or a litter. Carrot not included.

The Wooden Pie

This vehicle is for people looking to take a bite, or a slice, out of life. Fits four and twenty blackbirds, or scouts, if they squish together. Blueberry rhubarb, if anyone is asking. Ice cream on the side.

The Wooden Shoe

Take the SHOE on the road with this stylish take on athletic wooden footwear. Designed in pine with a cushy cedar instep for bumpy roads and freshness, this shoe could be your next step in fitness. Holds so many kids, you won't know what to do. Laces included.

The Wooden Wig

Find driving a drag? Tired of being teased by promises of cool road trips and then finding out that you're going nowhere fast? Ready to be snatched? Get your runway on with this bouffant updo of a vehicle made from a mix of knotty pine and birch. Fits a bunch of queens.

The Wooden Rose

Wood a rose by any other name smell as sweet as this bouquet on wheels made out of cedar? I don't know. But it is gorgeous and can fit at least a dozen.

Surrounded by wooden visions of the future of transportation, Cassie had this to say: "For me, knowing Cassandra had to live in a world where no one saw what she saw, I think that must have been horrible. And honestly, for a long time, it made me hate wood, and horses, and anything wooden and horse-like. Then I had a vision, that I could turn this hard history into art. This collection represents the past, future, and present for my family. It is art and a vehicle for understanding."

JO IS ALWAYS IN THE KNOW!
(AND MAKING STUFF WITH SCIENCE.)

MEET JO!

☆ ☆ ☆

NUMBER OF BADGES: 31

FAVORITE BADGE: May the Forge Be with You

LAST BOOK READ: *The Quark: Uncensored*

FAVORITE UNIT OF MEASUREMENT: The nanometer!

FAVORITE TOOL: Blowtorch

FAVORITE SCIENTIST: Margaret Hamilton

SPECIALTIES: Physics, chemistry, mechanical engineering, mathematics, microbiology, metalwork

I enjoy data, observations, and the art of writing those things down in columns.

The following information was formatted into something more readable, at the request of April. A complete index of my research and collected observations (which totals 123 pages) is available upon request.

UP, UP, AND AWAY

by Jo

For a scientist, there is very little that cannot be explained. Science tells us that the unexplained is only something that we have yet to comprehend. Things that are mysterious or strange are only so because we have yet to study them, yet to observe and record, measure and learn.

There are times when it feels like being a Lumberjane is testing my resolve as a scientist, until I take a second and read a book (*The Biography of Marie Curie* is a favorite), and then I remember why I love being a Lumberjane.

Or one of the many reasons why I love being a Lumberjane.

I came to this camp as a scientist. Being a Lumberjane is making me a better scientist.

Not just because of the fact that, in my time as a Lumberjane, I have developed more than a dozen patents for things that fly, swim, see farther and go faster—inventions I have developed in response to our adventures as scouts—but also because being a Lumberjane has challenged me to hone my observational skills, to consider new ways to understand and observe the world around me.

For my contribution to the BEAST, I studied three creatures linked by their connection to flight (a subject I have a personal interest in as the child of rocket scientists and an avid fan of aerodynamics and mechanical engineering). These creatures exist in worlds that should make sense to me—air, water, and space—and yet they don't. I cannot completely explain the worlds these creatures live in yet. But I will. Because that's what scientists do.

I am grateful to my fellow scouts for taking me to new and strange places, and for giving me an opportunity to challenge what I already understand about the world, and for pushing me to learn more.

RESEARCH UNIT #4534: UNICORNS

by *Jo*

CREATURE CATEGORY: Mystical Land Mammal

DANGER LEVEL: 3

FLIGHT ABILITY: 6

HABITAT: Remote pastures and plains

DIET: Clow bells

FAVORITE CATCHPHRASE: Neigh!

CREATURE PEEVES: Loud noises, drought, thistles, dog whistles

Possible official scientific terminology for the unicorn: *Equus cornu unum, Equus magicis, Foetida est cornu unum equum*

Cool words used to describe groups of unicorns: a disco, a rainbow, a party, a glitter, a hornucopia.

Τhe unicorn is a magical, mythological creature, a figure of fantasy films, a silhouette on sparkly lunch boxes, and also a very curious creature with several unique features.

One approach to studying the unicorn is to consider what other creatures we can compare it to. The most obvious candidate is the *Equus caballus*, or common horse. Like horses, unicorns appear to be herbivores, which means they eat only plants. Their hooves indicate that they are members of the Equidae family, which is to say that unicorns, like horses, have an odd number of toes, which is to say one HOOF toe per foot.

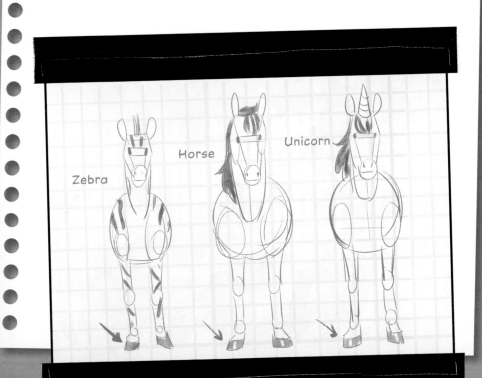

Zebra

Horse

Unicorn

While zebras are distinct members of the Equidae family owing to their black and white coats, the unicorn is distinct in that it has a single horn, often white, at the center of its forehead. The unicorn derives its name from this single (uni-) horn.

Like the common horse, unicorns come in several sizes. This researcher has observed unicorns varying from four to sixteen hands high.

A hand is a unit for measuring horses. It is the equivalent of four inches.

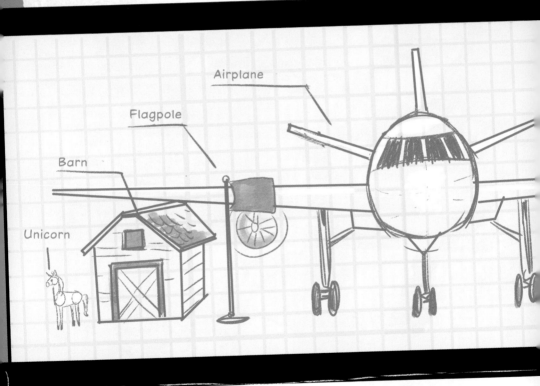

All of these features are certainly enough to include the unicorn in the annals of cool and mysterious creatures. For myself, as a scientist, one feature stands out that has less to do with aesthetics and more to do with what I can only describe as a curious, indescribable twist on aerodynamics and, frankly, physics: Unicorns can FLY. Without wings.

For context, most of the other animals on earth that can fly without wings, including the flying squirrel (Sciuridae family) and flying lizard (*Draco blanfordii*) are considerably smaller than the average unicorn. Also, almost all flying animals possess some sort of webbing that acts like a wing. Something unicorns do not possess.

There are several possible explanations for the unicorns' flight abilities.

Theory #1

The first explanation hypothesized by this researcher was that unicorns, like birds, might have hollow bones, which would make them surprisingly light. This hypothesis was obliterated when I and my fellow cabinmates attempted to move the unicorn for the first time and discovered it was so heavy as to be IMMOVABLE. My current estimate is that unicorns likely weigh as much as the average horse, which is about one thousand pounds. So probably no hollow bones.

This supercool ability was first observed by the members of Roanoke cabin while on a woodland walk at the beginning of an awesome UNICORN POWER! adventure, where they discovered not only unicorns and clow bells but also a mountain that didn't really exist and Cloudies (see page 58).

Theory #2

It is further possible that the unicorn is able to make itself incredibly heavy and incredibly light on demand, possibly through some internal chemistry. This hypothesis has yet to be pursued.

Theory #3

Another theory involves the unicorn's diet, which appears to consist only of a flower identified as a CLOW BELL. Clow bells, which only grow in forests and appear to be eaten only by unicorns, might provide some sort of fuel or chemical reaction that would allow unicorns to fly.

One way to call a unicorn is to take a clow bell and hold it up to a breeze. The ringing dinging sound can call a unicorn to any remote place, in case you're in kind of a fix and you need a ride! Another way to call a unicorn is to shout, "HEY! UNICORN." But this method doesn't really work.

Also worth noting is the unicorn's unique flight path: a zigzag pattern. Observations revealed that, ten times out of ten, unicorns adopted a zigzag pattern, even if this was the least productive means to travel between point A and point B.

It is possible that this pattern of flight has something to do with whatever force it is that keeps unicorns afloat. More study is required.

Another factor to consider is the olfactory element associated with unicorns, which admittedly makes them a little unpleasant to be around. Unicorns smell—let us say, subjectively—not good. It is difficult to assess whether this has to do with their diet, their environment, or if it is a defensive measure. If it is the latter, it's very effective.

↑

Unicorns smell like a piece of cheese that was locked in the back of a car and then left there for a decade, and then sprayed with a can of old sock.

In summary: Best enjoyed from a distance, unicorns are a very special part of the Lumberjane ecosystem. I, for one, am grateful to have experienced their strange odor and soared in their numbers. Current research reveals that more research is required to understand the nature of unicorns and unicorn flight. Next steps include locating more fields of clow bells and inventing a mask to block the unicorn smell.

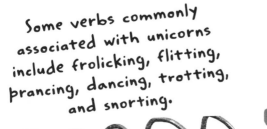

Some verbs commonly associated with unicorns include frolicking, flitting, prancing, dancing, trotting, and snorting.

RESEARCH UNIT #4535: CLOUDIES

by *Jo*

CREATURE CATEGORY: Airborne Phenomenon

DANGER LEVEL: 1

MOISTURE LEVEL: Dense

HABITAT: The clouds

DIET: Tea

FAVORITE CATCHPHRASE: Anything involving a mention of the weather

CREATURE PEEVES: Rain, lack of tea

Possible official scientific terminology for the Cloudies:

Nubes hominem,
Homo tempestas,
Condensatione hominem.

The Cloudies are an exceptional community of cloud-oriented creatures that live in the clouds.

The Cloudies were first encountered by the scouts of Roanoke cabin (myself included) on a trek up a mountain that, in retrospect, did not exist insomuch as upon our reaching the top of the mountain the mountain was no longer a mountain. This adventure also involved unicorns (see previous entry).

Based on the Law of Conservation of Matter (which states that matter, like a mountain, cannot be created or destroyed within an isolated system), it would seem difficult to suggest that, without a giant bulldozer or earthquake or other seismic interference, a mountain could just . . . disappear. Transform, yes (with considerable external influence, which, again, was not witnessed by this writer). Disappear, no.

A seemingly science-defying feature of the Cloudies is that they live in the clouds.

This is a phenomenon of note because a cloud is a floating form of water droplets. Water in the air turns into a gas, called water vapor, which, as it gets higher in the sky, cools and sticks to bits of dust, ice, or sea salt. Clouds can take many forms, none of which are generally thought to be habitable.

It is difficult to explain how it is that a community of quirky weather fanatics ended up living in the clouds. In fact, if anything, knowing exactly what a cloud is would make it impossible to believe that anything COULD live in a cloud, which, as we said, is made up of tiny water droplets, frozen crystals, or other particles, which—unlike the solid matter your house is constructed from and sits on—shouldn't be able to support anything.

Cirrocumulus and cirrus clouds tend to form above 18,000 feet.

Altocumulus and altostratus clouds are midlevel clouds.

Cumulonimbus clouds stretch from the ground to way up in the sky.

The more familiar clouds are cumulus (fluffy), stratus (blanket), and stratocumulus (waves or lines).

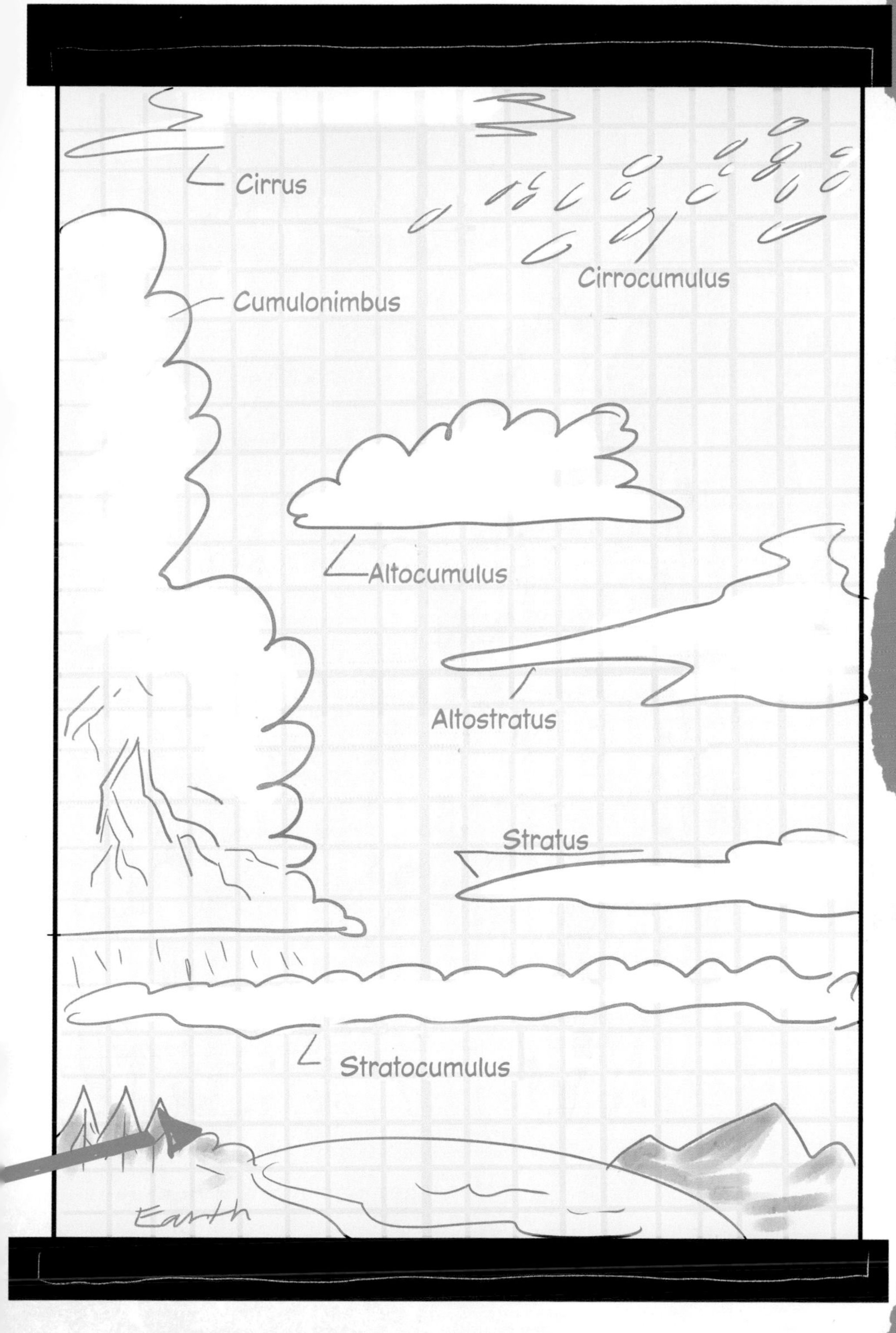
Cirrus
Cirrocumulus
Cumulonimbus
Altocumulus
Altostratus
Stratus
Stratocumulus
Earth

If they did, you wouldn't be able to fly THROUGH a cloud in an airplane, which you can.

If they did, they wouldn't be able to dissipate and move with the wind, which they do.

Moving on.

After a thorough discussion of the matter, the Cloudies could not explain how it is they live in the clouds. Which is to say that, if you try to ask them about it, they will change the subject, which makes me think it is possibly rude to ask. I think they have lived in the clouds for some time, though, as there is currently still residing with the Cloudies a former Lumberjane who is almost as old as the camp itself.

There are a few notable characteristics that all Cloudies have in common.

Lady Dana Deveroe Anastasia Mistytoe, who is also, she would want me to add, the greatest record holder in the history of the Lumberjanes, has been residing with the Cloudies for longer than she can remember. Not that you can ask her how long specifically, because she's not really into questions. Specifically, YOUR questions.

1. **Cloudies all have silky, glorious beards,** which they grow very long (generally waist length) and enjoy twirling and braiding and, sometimes, wrapping around their necks like a scarf.

2. **Cloudies all wear bathrobes.** It is unclear where they procure these, but they all wear them, tied at the waist. Flannel is preferred, in various shades of white and off-white. Apparently, there was one Cloudie who once wore a green bathrobe, which was considered by the Cloudies to be a very silly thing.

3. **Cloudies all like tea.** More specifically, Cloudies like drinking what they call tea, but which is not actually

the typical tea made from the leaf of a plant. What the Cloudies call tea is, from my assessment, very cold water, which they drink in what appear to be porcelain teacups. (Also not clear on where the Cloudies get these cups. They are generally very old cups. Very used, as well, as the Cloudies drink tea at several points throughout the day.)

4. **Cloudies love, LOVE, talking about the weather.** The Cloudie language is heavily influenced by climate-related terminology. Including:

Sunshine/Sunny (*adj.*)
- pleasing
- positive
- ex.: "It's so sunshine to see you!"

Foggy (*adj.*)
- kind of a bummer
- ex.: "It's a foggy thing, losing your teacup. A foggy thing indeed."

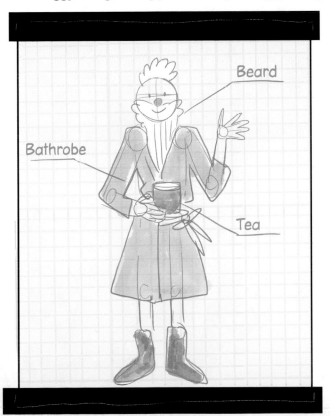

Cloudy (*adj.*)

- unclear
- typical
- ex. #1: "I'm a little cloudy on that. Maybe check in tomorrow."
- ex. #2: "It's a very cloudy thing, to drink tea."

Rainy (*adj.*)

- sad or unfortunate
- ex.: "Missing tea is a super rainy day."

Thunder (*adj.*)

- catastrophic, disorienting
- ex.: "Missing tea can be thunder for a Cloudie's day."

Rainbow (*adj.*)

- coming through something hard toward something better
- ex.: "She was having a hard time, but now she's having tea and feeling much rainbow."

In summary: Up until very recently, it was uncommon for Cloudies to comprehend, let alone discuss, the mechanics of the weather, including the logistics of lightning and how clouds are formed. Further research is clearly warranted to see how an understanding of the weather will affect the Cloudies' use of weather terminology. It is possible that knowing how clouds are formed would not be a good thing, as it is possibly not good to know you exist in an impossible state. I do believe further study of their unique linguistic patterns might be fruitful and enlighten us as to a possible connection between mind-set and matter.

This year the Cloudies celebrated their 144th This Is the Tea festival of teas with the introduction of their newest beverage, the Cloudy Fog.

RESEARCH UNIT #4536: MOON MICE

by Jo

CREATURE CATEGORY: Lunar Rodent

DANGER LEVEL: 5

HABITAT: Outer space

DIET: Cheese

Possible official scientific terminology for the moon mouse: Mus luna, Mus spatio iter faciebat

FAVORITE CATCHPHRASE: Over the moon.

CREATURE PEEVES: Cats, lack of cheese, spaceship motor problems

Many of us first became acquainted with the concept of the moon in children's books and from looking out our windows at the gradually disappearing and reappearing moon in the night sky. Astronomers and other space and science nerds know that in addition to the Earth's moon, there are millions upon billions of other moons to be found in the unimaginably vast stretches of space, which is really such a crowded place that sometimes it blows one's mind just to think of it.

What is a moon anyway? A moon is an astral body that orbits a planet or asteroid. They are generally made of rock and ice. While astronomers have spent the last several decades documenting the many moons in the galaxy, there are so so so so so many more yet to be discovered, which is why astronomers work such long hours.

No one knows how crowded outer space can be better than the moon pirates, a community of moon mice who, for generations, have sailed the celestial seas in search of treasure and, whenever possible, moon cheese. Moon pirates are probably the least well-documented members of the complex world of pirates, second only to cat pirates and hippo pirates (about whom almost nothing has been written—in fact, this sentence doubles the amount currently written about them).

The members of Roanoke cabin were first introduced to moon mice when a very precocious moon mouse named Castor, daughter of Captain Elara, landed in the camp and promptly started nibbling away at Kzyzzy's larder of cheeses. Fortunately, after stealing a very inedible foam moon, Castor was introduced to the wonders of being a Lumberjane and quickly became a treasured, if brief, member of Roanoke cabin.

Moon mice stand, on average, about six to twenty inches taller than non-moon mice. Aside from their size, they have the physiology and biology of Earth rodents, possibly most similar in size and proportion to those in the genus *Rattus*, with the exception that unlike Earth mice and rats, moon mice stand upright on their back legs.

On Earth, rats and mice in the wild eat insects and seeds, although in captivity, both are known for having a varied and complex diet. Moon mice eat cheese, with a preference for moon cheese, as found on the surface of various moons and in the various kitchens and larders of the places they land.

Castor said moon cheese tastes like regular Earth cheese, but cheesier.

One of the most distinguishing characteristics of moon mice is their penchant for adventure. Moon mice spend most of their time flying through the galaxy in ships helmed by daring captains, like Captain Elara. Captain Elara is the fifth of her family to lead the moon pirates, and Elara herself has helmed her ship for many, many years.

Captain Elara has a million gold rings on her tail and at least six on each of her claws and around her wrists. She likes a fluffy collar and puffy sleeves and a hat that is at least as wide as her arms. She looks like a super-fancy Musketeer and it is super cool!

Captain Elara's ship, the *Luna*, has sailed to stars, moons, and planets for generations and actually looks quite a bit like a moon from the outside. With very little information and not a lot of time to view their ships, I can report that the ships are aerodynamically curious and that they run on what Captain Elara described as "mouse moon power."

Due to proprietary restrictions it was outside the purview of this study to discuss the details of Elara's ship.

Because of her hectic schedule, Captain Elara rarely has time for interviews. A situation that is currently even more chaotic due to some intense negotiations with the moon moles. However, when she and Castor stopped by camp recently for Miss Qiunzella's annual Life Is Gouda cheese fest (the cheesiest fest in the world), I took the opportunity to ask her impressions of some of her most curious moons.

While I attempted to discuss some of my favorite moons, including Saturn's Titan and Pluto's Charon, Captain Elara was clearly bored by mention of what she referred to as "very basic celestial topography."

"Certainly," she said, munching on crackers and Brie, "those are moons. I don't know if I would describe them as moons of any *note*. But yes, they are moons. Was that all you wanted to talk about?"

I asked if there were any moons she did think were of note. She ate some more cheese and said there were thousands upon thousands.

I asked her to narrow it down.

Moon moles are steadfast, not-very-talkative creatures who prefer to spend most of their time burrowing into various moon crusts in search of cheese. They are very mole-like, aside from their size, which is about ten times larger than the average adult Earth mole.

And so, below, are ten moons Captain Elara described as falling into the category of Curious.

Captain Elara's Curious Moons

Blue Moon: "The most fabulous, stinky, tart cheese rivers of any planet I've ever seen. I could spend a week there with a bottle of cheese brandy and a thinly sliced apple."

Puppy Moon: "A very slobbery moon coated in hair. Very loud. The only universal source of puppy power, a fuel that allows us to kick the *Luna* into high gear for twenty minutes."

Steve: "I did not name Steve, but it is a solid source of cheddar."

Standing Moon Only: "A very popular moon."

Milk Moon: "Exactly as it sounds, perfectly creamy and delicious. Divine really. Enjoyed hot or cold."

Moon in the Middle: "Sometimes a difficult moon to pin down, as moons do move, but certainly a nice moon in a pinch."

Candy Moon: "Sickly sweet, but certainly a fabulous moon if you have that sort of tooth."

Harvest Moon: "Very chill, a kind of wood-fire-and-flannel type of moon."

Not a Minute Too Moon: "A relatively tardy moon."

March to a Different Moon: "A very stubborn moon. Some call it flashy. A little odd, if you ask me."

In summary: Moon mice are a unique and curious species that introduced me to an entirely new view of space as a place to be explored not just by scientists but by adventurers. The moon mice are complex and adaptive, having developed a means to acquire what they need from an unlikely source. I have the utmost respect for Elara and her crew and wish them the best journey on the high seas of space. I very much hope one day they'll tell me how that amazing ship works.

Don't hold your whiskers!
—Captain Elara

BARNEY REPORTING FOR DUTY!

MEET
BARNEY!

☆ ☆ ☆

NUMBER OF BADGES: 42

(SCOUTING LAD BADGES: 55**)**

FAVORITE BADGE: Better Safety Than Sorry!

LAST BOOK READ: *45,345 Uses for a Piece of String That Could Save Your Life*

FAVORITE SAFETY TOOL: My brain!

FAVORITE KNOT: Figure 9 Loop

FAVORITE ACCESSORY: Neckerchief

SPECIALTIES: Water safety, fire safety, animal safety, anthropology, knots, survival skills, wilderness skills

I enjoy scout safety because it helps me keep my fellow scouts safe while we experience the rich wilderness around us.

WATCH OUT!
by Barney

As a Lumberjane, I see it as my duty to always be prepared. Being a scout, I am lucky to have the time and resources to learn about land, sea, and sky, and the creatures and the plants you find there.

One of my favorite parts of being a scout is acquiring the knowledge I need not just to be personally ready for any situation, but also to help my fellow scouts when they need it.

This summer, I was fortunate to get the chance to share my understanding with my fellow scouts to help them be safe. Water safety, like all forms of safety, is about learning the best way to enjoy a place in a way that keeps you and your fellow scouts free from harm.

Doing this project also made me think about how much of safety involves understanding that there is always more going on in the world around you than what appears at first glance. There are hidden dangers, sure, but also other creatures to consider. Water safety is about staying alert, and in some cases staying away from carnivorous hunters, but it's also about being considerate of an environment that is home to a world of organisms, most of which you can't even see. Reading through this report and seeing all the amazing life-forms my fellow scouts have researched, I'm inspired to learn more. The more you know, the better you can be considerate to all living things!

I am pleased to share my knowledge of some very interesting creatures in this project. I learned so much working on this, and I had fun, which is the Lumberjane way!

IF YOU DON'T WANT TO BE DINO-SORRY, READ THIS!

by Barney

CREATURE CATEGORY:
Prehistoric Threats

WATCH OUT! LEVEL: *9*

ANCIENT LEVEL: *10*

HABITATS: *Tropical and mountain climates and beyond magical portals*

DIET: *Carnivorous*

FAVORITE CATCHPHRASE: *RAAARRR!*

CREATURE PEEVES: *Ice ages*

Despite being extinct for between 243 and 233.23 million years, dinosaurs, when they appear at camp or any other place in the present day, should always be considered a serious threat. Even if they're supposed to be extinct.

Dinosaurs are dangerous because:

1. They are generally very large (raptors, for example, are roughly forty feet long and weigh about nine tons).
2. They have large teeth.
3. They have claws.
4. The ones that are carnivorous eat meat (which includes humans).

Despite seeming to be VERY different in many ways, dinosaurs, theropod dinosaurs in particular, are actually the ancestors of BIRDS. Both have hollow bones, three-toed limbs, and wishbones!

So maybe you should keep an eye out for that angry chicken!

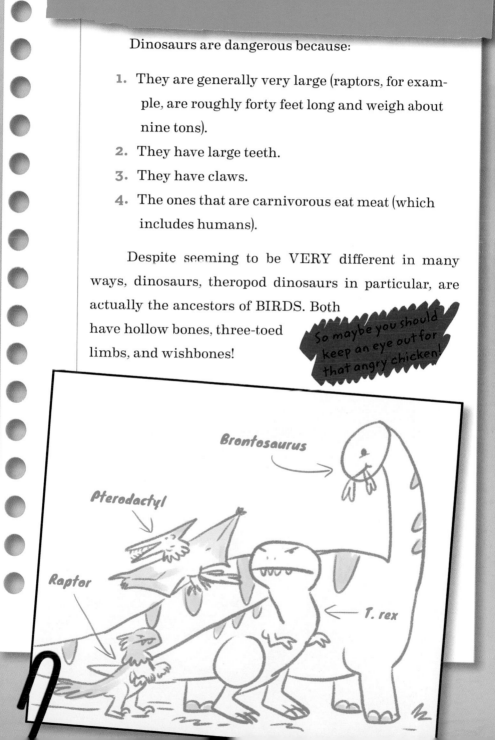

Brontosaurus

Pterodactyl

Raptor

T. rex

The most important thing to know about dinosaurs is this: Not all dinosaurs are dangerous, but those that are dangerous are EXTREMELY dangerous. If a dangerous, carnivorous dinosaur catches you, it is very possible it will eat you.

This is obviously a sobering if not terrifying thought. However, if we use our heads, it is a fate that can be easily avoided by following a few basic rules.

1. Do Not Feed

It is a common practice for people to attempt to feed wild animals. This is not good for animals or for people. Feeding wild animals messes with their diet and interrupts the way they normally do things. Feeding a dinosaur is doubly dangerous, because a dinosaur would always rather eat a scout than your leftover sandwich.

2. Do Not Pat/Photograph/Talk to a Dinosaur

Do not for any reason attempt to make contact with or attempt to photograph a dinosaur. There is a habit among scouts to want to document their encounters with local wildlife (whether for badges or recreational purposes). But a dinosaur is not a squirrel. It is a threat. It will not consider a photo or a kind word a form of flattery. It will just eat you.

Related Badge Skill:
SNAP!

3. Do Not Go to Places Where Dinosaurs Are

The main thing to keep in mind when dealing with creatures like the dinosaur is to avoid them. If there is a spot on a map marked as being the habitat of a dinosaur, you should avoid that area. If you hear a dinosaur, you should immediately vacate the area in the opposite direction.

Related Badge Skill:
RIGHT ON TRACK

4. Do Not Underestimate a Dinosaur

There are several reasons one might underestimate or misjudge a dinosaur. For example, the T. rex's particularly small arms in relation to the size of its body give people a radical misunderstanding of the dinosaur's capability to capture its prey. Rest assured, the T. rex does not rely on its small limbs to grab its next snack. One might also underestimate a dinosaur due to the fact that dinosaurs are technically extinct, a victim of (some theorize) the Ice Age. Of course, all scouts must come to terms with the fact that just because something is very improbable does not mean precautions should not be taken.

Stay safe!

Other theories suggest that the extinction of the dinosaurs was caused by a giant asteroid or a volcano! These theories obviously do not consider the possibility of other dimensions and Greek gods.

For whatever reason, scientific theories are not always the most helpful when on a Lumber-adventure.

CARNIVOROUS PLANTS

(PART 1)

by Barney

What are carnivorous plants?

Carnivorous plants are plants that trap their food, unlike most plants, which make their food through the amazing process of photosynthesis, a process that is as fun to do as it is to spell. There are more than five hundred known species of carnivorous plants, and there are plants that have some, but not all, features of carnivorousness.

There are a variety of ways that carnivorous plants trap their food, including snap traps, bladder traps, and pitfall traps. Most of the food trapped by carnivorous plants are insects, as in the case of the bugs caught and absorbed by the well-known Venus flytrap.

Most carnivorous plants are not a danger to scouts. In fact, like most plant life, it is more the actions of scouts, who should be careful where they tread, that could jeopardize carnivorous plants.

If you find a carnivorous plant in the wild, leave it be! In addition to being possibly dangerous, they're also relatively rare and will live longer if you leave them in their natural surroundings.

CARNIVOROUS PLANTS

(PART 2)

CREATURE CATEGORY: *MEGA Flora*

WATCH OUT! LEVEL: *9*

HABITAT: *Other dimensions*

DIET: *Big things that wander into their traps*

FAVORITE CATCHPHRASE: *SNAP!*

CREATURE PEEVES: *Insecticides*

This is a carnivorous flower I am currently calling the SUPER CARNIVORE.

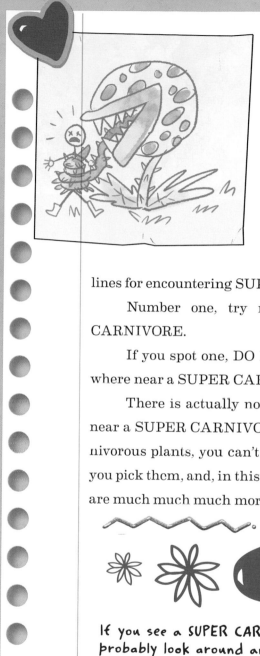

SUPER CARNIVORES can be upward of ten feet tall and their flowers are bigger than basketballs. Their mouths are big enough to fit a bicycle. If you stand next to a SUPER CARNIVORE to see if it's as tall as you, that might be the last thing you do.

Here are a few guidelines for encountering SUPER CARNIVORES.

Number one, try not to encounter a SUPER CARNIVORE.

If you spot one, DO NOT, no matter what, go anywhere near a SUPER CARNIVORE.

There is actually no reason at all to go anywhere near a SUPER CARNIVOROUS flower. Like other carnivorous plants, you can't eat them, they die as soon as you pick them, and, in this case, SUPER CARNIVORES are much much much more likely to snap YOU up.

Pick a daisy instead! Or a radish. Radishes are yummy!

If you see a SUPER CARNIVORE, also, you should probably look around and make sure you're not accidentally backing into something else super dangerous because SUPER CARNIVORES are not an everyday kind of thing. They're like a "HOLY COW" kind of thing.

STONE GUARDIANS: LET'S GET READY TO RUBBLE!

by Barney

CREATURE CATEGORY: *Mystical Mineral*

WATCH OUT! LEVEL: *7*

GAME LEVEL: *12*

HABITAT: *Places where things are being guarded (see also: caves, underground tunnels, castles)*

DIET: *None*

FAVORITE CATCHPHRASES: *WHO GOES THERE? PREPARE FOR BATTLE!*

CREATURE PEEVES: *Chisels, losing*

Although it is difficult to determine the exact origin of the stone guardians, one thing we can say for sure about this set of noble foes is that they are not to be messed with.

Loomingly tall, at an average of fifteen feet, and made of rock with chiseled humanoid features (like statues), stone guardians are employed by Greek deities to guard treasures and other secret things. Due to the nature of this employment, they are generally found in caves or at entrances decorated with elaborate stone carvings. They are powerful and intimidating and prone to displaying magnificent feats of strength. *AKA showing off*

The safety conscious would do well to avoid an encounter with a stone guardian, which should really only come up if you've managed to locate something like, for example, a magical stone with properties that you pursue for reasons of curiosity and a love of adventure.

ADVENTURE RULES!

If you do come upon a stone guardian, the only thing you can do, beyond running away very quickly, which is not always possible, is to best the guardian in a test of strength. The following are several options suggested by the scouts of Roanoke cabin, with possible pitfalls and benefits.

1. April: Arm Wrestling

Should only be attempted if: You are actually really good at arm wrestling (I am).

Benefits: This is a solid slam dunk of a show of strength and all it requires is your massive arm muscles and an understanding that most arm wrestling is grit and physics and not muscle.

Possible downside: It's not the most fun in the world to grip a giant stone hand, so if you're a little sensitive of palm, maybe not for you.

2. Molly: Thumb War

Should only be attempted if: You have strong thumbs.

Benefits: Again, this is something that even someone less than a quarter as tall as a stone guardian can attempt as a battle of strength and is more about speed and thumb control than might.

Possible downside: Smushed thumb.

3. Mal: Staring Contest

Should only be attempted if: You don't think you'll blink.

Benefits: A feat of strength isn't just about muscles, it's about will, and this is something that will very likely throw a stone guardian off their game, because back in the days when the Greek gods championed over the world, there weren't a lot of these.

Possible downside: A slight headache from keeping your eyes open.

4. Hes: Hot-Dog-Eating Contest

Should only be attempted if: You have access to a lot of hot dogs.

Benefits: Sometimes a strong stomach is your best bet. If you happen, like Ripley, to have a skill for putting away vast amounts of food, why not use that to your advantage?

Possible downside: Stomachache.

5. Ripley: Dance Dance Contest

Should only be attempted if: You can lure a stone guardian into an arcade.

Benefits: Wouldn't it be amazing? You and the stone guardian of your choosing going toe to toe on an electronic dance floor grooving to the beat of a crazy K-pop number? I mean, maybe it's not possible, but I think it would be so cool.

Possible downside: There probably isn't an arcade big enough for a stone guardian, but a scout can dream.

Another means of defeating the stone guardians is to know your math. In our adventure we were able to escape the tomb by knowing the Fibonacci sequence, in which each number is the sum of the two preceding numbers, starting from 0 and 1.

MAL TO
THE MAX!

MEET MAL!

☆ ☆ ☆

NUMBER OF BADGES: 23

FAVORITE BADGES: Guitar It On, Bang the Drum

LAST BOOK READ: *What the Actual Joan Jett: The Joan Jett Story*

FAVORITE BANDS: Sleater-Kinney, Le Tigre, the Black Hearts, Bikini Kill (full list available upon request)

FAVORITE INSTRUMENT: Electric guitar

FAVORITE GAME: Scavenger hunt!

SPECIALTIES: Strategy, guitar, vocals, composition, hair

I'm never sure what we're supposed to say in these things. How about LUMBERJANES ROCK! That should do it.

CURIOUS CREATURES DOING AMAZING THINGS

by MAL

To me, being a Lumberjane is about embracing all the parts of my personality. Like, I'm a musical person, but I'm obsessed with puzzles, too, and I'm the best capture-the-flag player I know. Like, if you put a flag out there, I'm going to capture it, for sure.

Being a Lumberjane is also about all the things I didn't think I was going to like that I actually like. Like macramé, who knew? Even drama class. I'm so into it, I might even take a mime badge!

The creatures I interviewed are also good examples of going beyond expectations. They're creatures you might think of one way, but that's not all they're about. Like, ghosts who didn't even know what an electric guitar was at the beginning of the summer rocking out!

One of the coolest things about all these creatures is that they're more than just a category. Each of these creatures is a story. They're not just ghosts and selkies, they're ghosts and selkies marching to the beat of their own drum.

Anyway, this was super fun. I hope we get our BEAST, but even if we don't, I had a great time doing this! I'm even starting a werewolf meditation class. Thanks!

DAEDALUS RULEZ!

A MIXTAPE REPORT

by MAL

CREATURE CATEGORY: Phantom Furies

DANGER LEVEL: 3

ROCKING-OUT LEVEL: 9

HABITAT: The night

FAVORITE CATCHPHRASE: BOO!

CREATURE PEEVES: Daylight, things that are heavy, bad ghost stories

For as long as there have been camps and scouts and bonfires, there have been stories about ghosts. They're called ghost stories.

Related Badge Skill:
IF YOU GOT IT, HAUNT IT

Ghost stories are stories about ghosts, generally doing spooky things and just overall BEING spooky. These stories are meant to scare the scouts who hear them, so then they'll lie curled up in their sleeping bags at night, wondering if every sound they hear outside their window is a ghoul looking to steal their ears. Or something.

It makes sense that ghosts are the subject of stories meant to scare. After all, ghosts are sort of see-through, and they only show up at night.

At the same time, ghosts are also pretty cool, because they're see-through, and they only show up at night.

Fortunately, Miss Qiunzella Thiskwin Penniquiqul Thistle Crumpet's Camp for Hardcore Lady Types has some of the coolest ghosts around, and they're working hard to shake up our ideas about what it means to be a spirit.

Just to make sure we're covering the facts, ghosts are dead. Which is to say, before ghosts were ghosts, they were alive, and now they are dead. Ghosts are technically the manifestation or spirit of a person who used to be alive. There are many different kinds of ghosts, including kitchen ghosts and cabin ghosts, most relevant for our purposes here.

In addition to the ghosts of Daedalus cabin, Miss Qiunzella Thiskwin Penniquiqul Thistle Crumpet's Camp for Hardcore Lady Types also has a kitchen ghost named Inez who is a vegetarian and prefers her snacks to be delivered by BunBun, daughter of camp cook, Kzyzzy.

Roanoke's introduction to the Lumberghosts of Daedalus cabin was spawned when one of the ghosts named Claudia attempted to make contact with Roanoke cabin by stealing Mal's socks. This adventure turned out well, but Lumberjanes alive and dead are advised that stealing is not an acceptable way to get someone's attention.

After being dead for several decades and overcoming a somewhat rocky reintroduction to camp "life," the Lumberghosts of Daedalus devoted themselves to camp activities. Although ghosts can only really participate in activities once the sun has left the sky, Daedalus has not let that stand in their way of being the best ghost scouts they can be.

Ghosts, who are not made of solid matter, can actually dive headfirst into solid objects, which makes them great mechanics, specifically Heddie. Recently, Heddie and I invented a new form of headlamp that runs on lunar (rather than solar) power, which was used in the Lumberjane All Night Long volleyball and dance tournament.

Related Badge Skill:

UP ALL NIGHT

After earning several badges, Daedalus decided they needed to find something they could all do together that would also combat some of the negative campfire-sourced stereotypes some scouts still had about ghosts. "Scouts should know that just because you're dead doesn't mean you can't rock out," Maggie explained while backstage at their last concert.

"We understand that people think ghosts are boring and only listen to classical music," Deborah added while simultaneously tuning her bass, "and we DO enjoy classical music, and swing, but being dead doesn't mean you stop listening to NEW things!"

And so PHANTOM MAIDENS was born (dead).

This band, a power trio, consists of the current members of Daedalus cabin, who would like to be known as: Mayhem Maggie on drums, Deadly Deborah on bass, and Heddie Headbanger on guitar and vocals.

Other cool (alive) power trios:
Rush, Le Tigre, Sleater Kinney, The Police

Currently, the band plays mostly covers. However, Mayhem Maggie, who is the lone songwriter of the group, has begun penning some songs of her own, with titles including: "Scout the Dead Girl," "Sock It to Me," "Dead in the Woods," and the promising "BOO YOU WHO!"

Lead singer Heddie is always looking for new inspiration. "I love your music collection," Heddie said, referring to this reporter's pretty awesome selection of tunes. "There's this band, Queen? Amazing. At first, I thought it was the actual queen singing, and it's not. It's much better."

First of all, Queen *is* a lovely band, and PHANTOM MAIDENS is currently developing a cover of their hit "Who Wants to Live Forever."

Suffice to say, PHANTOM MAIDENS proves that shredding guitar and destroying on drums isn't just for the living. This reporter is looking forward to their next concert with bated breath.

PHANTOM MAIDEN'S HARDCORE COVERS SET LIST
Dead Scouts (Joy Division)
Happy Phantoms Go to Camp (Tori Amos)
Who Wants to Live Forever at Camp (Queen)
The Ghost of Your Camp Counselor (My Chemical Romance)
Drum solo
Walking with a Ghost Scout (Tegan and Sara)
The Ghost in Your Cabin (Psychedelic Furs)
All My Afterlife (Foo Fighters)
After Dark Is Our Favorite Time (Le Tigre)

SHARIN' WITH SEAFARIN' KAREN

by MAL

CREATURE CATEGORY: Shape-Shifting Mammal

DANGER LEVEL: 3

HABITAT: Ports and ships, or land near water if necessary

DIET: Mixed

FAVORITE CATCHPHRASE: Shipshape!

CREATURE PEEVES: Bad knots, messy crews, selkies

Master of the seven seas, Nautical Instructor Seafarin' Karen is the face of seaworthy know-how at Miss Qiunzella Thiskwin Penniquiqul Thistle Crumpet's Camp for Hardcore

Lady Types, and she also just happens to be a shape-shifter, which is a creature with the ability to change form from human animal to a different animal.

This transformation can be instigated by the shape-shifter or triggered by the presence of an external element, like the moon, or extreme emotion.

In Seafarin' Karen's case, her animal form is a wolf (making her a "lycan" or "werewolf"), but shape-shifters can take a variety of forms (see Bearwoman's Breakfast Special, page 118, and Splash Splash, page 106, in this collection for other examples).

Some shape-shifters prefer to stay in their human form; others feel more comfortable in fur or scales. Seafarin' Karen generally spends her days on two legs, although when she needs to get from one side of camp to the other, she can often be seen sprinting through the trees in her wolf form.

Instructor Seafarin' Karen has been an invaluable member of the Lumberjane community. Though she started out the victim of the cackling selkies, she has been a fine teacher and, when required, contest judge.

The youngest of a litter of seven pups, Seafarin' Karen knew from a young age that life at sea was the life for her. Seafarin' Karen first got her paws wet serving as a shipmate on Pirate Gray Beard's ship, *The Good Ship Growl*. Seafarin' Karen describes Gray Beard as the best mentor a sailor could have. He taught her how to navigate her course by the same moon that caused Gray Beard to transform from a five-foot sailor into a seven-foot gray wolf.

PIRATE
GRAY BEARD

Related Badge Skill:
ALL FOR KNOT

Lately, in addition to her duties as the course instructor, Seafarin' Karen has taken over teaching mindfulness practice, a practice she calls "Tidal Meditation."

"Life on the high seas, as well as life at camp, can be very stressful," Seafarin' Karen explained. "There's a lot to manage. Also, I'm someone who likes things shipshape, so I can get a little . . . frustrated when things get messy."

For Seafarin' Karen, a short temper is a family feature. Like many werewolves, when she loses her head, things get hairy.

"Arrrr yes," Seafarin' Karen agreed, "obviously I have no issue with my werewolf self, but ideally a werewolf wants to change shape at will, not out of frustration."

This past year, Seafarin' Karen has found meditation to be an essential part of her daily practice.

"I'm a person who likes a schedule," Seafarin' Karen noted, "so I like a good morning meditation to get the day started right."

The key components to Tidal Meditation are as follows:

1. Find a comfortable spot. Sitting is fine (on a rock or a chair, on the grass or the beach).
2. Feel your feet or paws on the ground. Feel the rest of your body, whatever shape it might be in at the moment.
3. Take three deep breaths. In through the nose, out through the mouth. Panting acceptable.
4. Picture the ocean in its vastness, the blue sky. Imagine wet earth beneath your paws as you gallop through the forest.
5. Listen to the breeze floating past your ears.
6. Feel the sun on your fur/skin.
7. Take three more deep breaths.
8. Repeat deep breaths as long as you feel necessary.

An expert in knots and rope, Seafarin' Karen next hopes to take up pottery so she can decorate her meditation studio.

Related Badge Skill:
VIEW TO A KILN

Related Badge Skill:
PEACE AND QUILT

HERE HAIR EVERYWHERE

by MAL

CREATURE CATEGORY: Mystical Maned Mammal

DANGER LEVEL: 7

HABITAT: Mountain ranges and various climates
with a preference for cold

DIET: Vegetarian

FAVORITE CATCHPHRASE: You ain't seen nothing yeti.

CREATURE PEEVES: Burrs, humans, tangles, sunny days

The yeti are yet another example of the tried-and-true saying "Don't judge a book by its cover." Like many mythological creatures, yeti have a larger-than-life reputation, but are, when you meet them up close and personal, a cookie jar of complexity.

I was able to infiltrate a recent gathering of yeti this summer when they held their triannual hacky sack tournament in the Whispering Woods. I was invited to play because I can hacky sack like no one's business. Just sayin'.

Related Badge Skill:
SHAVE THE WAY

Kicking the hacky sack with the yeti, I was fascinated to learn about the yeti's new movement, FUR IS FABULOUS. Created by a group that calls itself Hair to Stay!

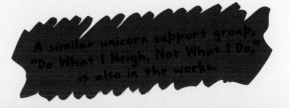

A similar unicorn support group, "Do What I Neigh, Not What I Do," is also in the works.

This movement calls upon yeti, Sasquatch, and all creatures who are very hairy to celebrate their unique looks and style. This movement is in opposition to a woodland trend of removing fur in order to adopt a newly fashionable hairless or "smoothie" look taken up by various yeti over the past summer, due to rumors that lots of body hair is uncool.

Admittedly, I had seen a flash of a large pink creature running in the woods and I wondered what was going on.

The following is an excerpt from the Fur Is Fabulous handout.

ABOMINABLE IS JUST A STATE OF MIND

Unfortunately, there are some creatures out there stuck in an abominable rut, in a pattern of negative thinking, with some yeti and Sasquatch saying that there's something wrong with being hairy, that there's something uncool about having furry legs or a fuzzy face.

There is nothing wrong with being bushy!

Shaggy is what we are!

FUR IS NATURAL!

Did you know all the things your fur does for you? It's more than just soft and fluffy. It keeps you warm when it's cold out by trapping heat between your skin and your fur. It's better than any sweater and it's FREE! It can even help you cool off when you overheat! Also, it protects you from the elements, like the sun and snow. Do you know how much yeti save on sunscreen? It's a lot! Humans only WISH they had our luxurious pelts.

FURRY LEGACY

We are the stuff of legend just the way we are. Don't let anyone tell you that you need to change who you are to be cool or fashionable. Who you are now is awesome.

Final riffs?

Some of the coolest music movements—the punks, the hippies, the mods—embraced a style that was outside of what people thought was okay, thereby defining a new cool. People yelled at hippies to cut their hair and told punks they looked crazy. But both these groups and looks prevailed!

Sometimes it's hard to love the parts that don't fit with the status quo. The parts that other people define as weird. Sometimes it takes a movement to get us to see those parts as special and unique instead of weird. I'm glad there are some yeti taking the fur-st step toward embracing their fuzz.

YETI TO THE MAX!

MOOSE GAIT

by MAL

CREATURE CATEGORY: Mammal

DANGER LEVEL: 5

HABITAT: The forest

DIET: Vegetarian

FAVORITE CATCHPHRASE: None

CREATURE PEEVES: Mosquitoes

Though not currently an Olympic sport, the art of moose dressage is a refined and fascinating discipline enjoyed by a legacy of Lumberjanes and moose.

The term "dressage" comes from the French word for "training," and it's both a way to train and a competition, practiced mostly with horses. The traditional equine art of dressage involves a series of specific movements and patterns. Horse and rider must work as one, moving smoothly, gracefully, and effortlessly around the arena in a set series.

Moose dressage, clearly, is this, with moose.

Related Badge Skill:
GET A MOOSE ON

Related Badge Skill:
BUST A MOOSE!

The fact that moose dressage is a practice in the Lumberjane world and not a part of any other world I could find in my research has, likely, something to do with the fact that moose have long held a very esteemed position at camp, stabled and trained by scouts and counselors.

Also: Our camp rules!

The original camp director of Miss Qiunzella Thiskwin Penniquiqul Thistle Crumpet's, Miss Qiunzella herself, was a hardcore moose fan and rider.

How she came to be a moose rider is difficult to say.

Knowing what I know about moose led me to ask myself, and others, several questions.

Did Miss Qiunzella have a pet moose before starting the camp? Did she discover a moose at some point during her duties? Where did she get the idea to RIDE a moose?

When I asked Rosie, an avid moose rider, about this, she suggested this question, like so many, was probably not one I would find the answer to so I should move on.

And so.

Dressage. One of the more curious elements of Lumberjane moose culture. Which is saying a lot.

Evidence located after extensive searching, including letters and some pretty detailed sketches, suggests that the art of moose dressage was developed by Miss Qiunzella Thiskwin Penniquiqul Thistle Crumpet. There is very little documentation on the inspiration for this sport's development, but there are many images of Miss Qiunzella with her beloved moose, Rupert Igor Bandyheart Devonshire Hasselhoof III, in the arena, going through their paces and looking very pleased.

Based on these sketches and graphs found in the library, we know that Miss Qiunzella replaced the top hat traditionally worn by dressage riders with a hat with a very large pom-pom. She did wear gloves, a fashion no longer observed by current moose riders, because current moose dressage riders find them fussy.

Today the grand moose dressage tradition is carried on by Rosie's prize moose, Jeremy, and Zodiac scout Hes, who is one of the more skilled moose riders at camp.

OTHER FAMOUS LUMBERJANE MOOSE DRESSAGE RIDERS:
Maybelle Harness Shetland Trotter III, riding Archibald
Danica Elaine Steps, riding Celine
Julia Ramona Steps, riding Moody

As part of her rigorous training, Hes spends many hours a day learning the standard elements of moose dressage routines, which are as follows:

The Moosey Lucy: a trot

The Iron Lady: a half turn

The Pom-Pom Slide: a right leg crossed
    over left type of thing

The Hurry Up: a canter

The Broad: a circle around half the arena

The Tall Board: a full loop around the complete arena

A Dear Deer: backing up the center of the arena

A Full Antler: a dead stop in the center of the arena

Other current moose in the Lumberjane stable: Joshua, Lucy, Sasha, and Brenda

Final riffs?

Hes told me that moose dressage has taught her to appreciate Jeremy and given her a greater understanding of moose behavior. Most specifically, moose dressage is only something you can do if the moose is feeling like it. If they are not feeling like it, they just stand there no matter what you do. Which is possibly why there are so few competitions.

Nevertheless, I am pleased to have spent time digging into this very curious little bit of Lumberjane history and its connection to this majestic member of the animal kingdom.

SPLASH SPLASH

by MAL

CREATURE CATEGORY: Shape-Shifting Water Mammal

DANGER LEVEL: 5

HABITAT: Bodies of water

DIET: Fish

FAVORITE CATCHPHRASE: SELKIES RULE!

CREATURE PEEVES: People stealing their skins, hecklers

I don't think there's anything harder than being funny. I hate water, and I'd rather swim in the ocean than stand onstage and try to make people laugh. Music, even if it's not GREAT, is at least a song. Humor is what they call subjective, which means it's REALLY hard to do, because things that some people find funny, other people really DON'T.

Unlike music, which is often said to soothe the savage beast, humor can easily ruffle feathers and then get you attacked by birds. So while it really takes guts to get up onstage and sing a song, it takes unbelievably tremendous courage, in my humble opinion, to get up onstage and try to make someone laugh. Which is exactly what selkies Bon, Moirin, Sunday, and Monday decided to do with their Selkies Stand-Up Comedy Hour.

Selkies, for those unfamiliar, are shapeshifters who can take both seal and human form, which they take by shedding their seal skins. If selkies lose their skin, or if it is taken, they cannot transform. Which causes them a great deal of stress, as you can imagine.

The selkies' original humor preference was for insult comedy, which is to say that they enjoy insulting people. They especially enjoyed calling land mammals things like "skinless barnacles" and "fleshy fish food" and "leg seals." This, however, was not very popular when they tried to get an audience.

"Yeah, no one liked it," Sunday grumbled when I interviewed the selkies. "You Lumberjanes don't like insults, I guess. So we decided to change it up."

Currently, the selkies have moved their act into a series of what they call "splash splash" jokes.

BON: Splash splash.
MOIRIN: Who's there?
BON: Wanda.
MOIRIN: Wanda who?
BON: You Wanda get my seal of approval,
    you better open this door.

MONDAY: Splash splash.
BON: Who's there?
MONDAY: Whale.
BON: Whale who?
MONDAY: Whale have you been?
    We've been waiting for hours!

Humor, as I said, is subjective.

Related Badge Skill:
PUNGEON MASTER

The selkies have also branched into fish jokes.

MONDAY: What did the goldfish say to the clownfish?
BON: What are you looking at, BOZO?!

BON: What did the octopus say to the dolphin?
MOIRIN: Nothing, cuz they don't speak dolphin!

While I don't necessarily think the selkies are the funniest magical beings I've ever encountered, I have respect for the fact that they are endlessly amused by their own jokes. No one is a bigger fan of the selkie comedy hour than the selkies, and they keep the place packed. They even wear Stand-Up for Selkies T-shirts and hats when they're not in seal form.

Final riffs?

We should all be our own biggest fans, even if that's being a fan of fishy splash splash jokes. The selkies told me they write the funniest fishy splash splash jokes, and even if that's true mostly because no one else is writing them, it is still true. So that's kind of awesome.

Currently you can enjoy the comedy stylings of the selkies on Thursday nights when the moon is up and the tide is high.

One creature you DON'T want in the audience for a stand-up show? Griffins. They hate comedy and react very badly to performances they don't like.

RIPLEY-RIFIC!

MEET RIPLEY!

☆ ☆ ☆

NUMBER OF BADGES: 35

FAVORITE BADGES: Hatch You Later, It's Poppin'

LAST BOOK READ: *Kittens, Kittens,* and *Even More Kittens*

FAVORITE BREAKFAST: Pancakes

FAVORITE PANCAKE: Chocolate chip

FAVORITE MANEUVER: ROCKET RIPLEY!

FAVORITE UNICORN: Mr. Sparkles

FAVORITE COLOR: Glitter

SPECIALTIES: High-energy movements in the form of dance or just general jumping, team spirit, kitten care

I can jump, bounce, and generally move very fast when required. I like glitter and things that sparkle!

WHY I LIKE CUTE AND MAGICAL THINGS
by RIPLEY

I like all kinds of things. I like big things and little things. Squishy things and sparkly things. I like things that smell like cinnamon toast and things that make your eyes water. I don't like things that give you a cold, but that's pretty much it. Oh, and I don't like things that give you hives. But that's it. I don't really think that one thing is better than another. Even a thing that gives you hives is just as good as a thing that smells like cotton candy.

ANYWAY.

I'm just trying to say that lots of things are really cool. So you shouldn't make one thing important and another thing NOT important. I think it is way better to have more of every-thing than worry about making one thing special. Like pancakes! How many pancakes is too many? We might never know.

Magical things are often described as special. I think magical things are maybe kind of special because they're kind of rare. Like the first time I saw a rain-bow in a rainy-day sky and realized

that the only time I would see a rainbow would be in that special kind of rainy-day sky, it made it all that much cooler. It even made me like rainy days.

For this project, I got to spend a lot of time with cute creatures. Which is maybe not special, but I felt very lucky, which is how I pretty much always feel as a Lumberjane. I think one thing this project made me think about is how lucky I am to spend time with cute creatures. Not that it would be so much worse to spend all your time with tax lawyers or sandcastle makers. Actually, that might be really cool.

Thank you to April, whose idea this was.

And thanks to Jen for not getting too too mad when I let the unicorn in the cabin last week.

ROC: A VERY BIG BIRD
by RIPLEY

CREATURE CATEGORY: Fantastic Fowl

DANGER LEVEL: 5

HABITAT: Nests, the sky, trees

DIET: Insects

FAVORITE CATCHPHRASE: SQUAWK!

CREATURE PEEVES: Small nests

 Arguably one of the most dynamic and thrilling sectors of zoology, ornithology, the study of birds and bird behaviors, opens up to scouts a dizzying array of feathered creatures, with so many to be found right here in the forests surrounding Miss Qiunzella Thiskwin Penniquiqul Thistle Crumpet's Camp for Hardcore Lady Types.

There are a lot of different birds a scout can spot in the woods and trees and lakes around camp. There are some birds that you need to sit very still to see and some you need to crawl up into a tree to see (sitting very still). You do not have to wait patiently to see very big birds like rocs, because they just show up when you're not expecting them and do very big things, like pick up a bus.

Before scouts like us knew about rocs, the biggest birds we knew about were the ostrich and the wandering albatross. Neither of these birds is big enough to pick up a bus.

A roc did actually visit Miss Qiunzella's and pick up a bus that happened to be full of camp directors. All camp directors were eventually returned safely to camp.

I was thrilled to be able to assist with the Lumber-rescue of the camp directors whose bus the roc abducted, which afforded me the opportunity to give chase on the back of Marigold, my giant kitten, and work with Roanoke to solve a problem and see a roc up close.

Roc

Ostrich

Based on the colors of its feathers, Barney and I have deduced that the roc we spotted near camp is probably related to the magpie family, and so we have for now named him a GIANT YELLOW-BILLED MAGPIE.

The giant magpie has black feathers and a bright yellow beak, like a school bus! The giant magpie has glowing blue eyes that look like they could do x-rays (although we don't know if they can).

Although it's hard to watch the magpie and still maintain a safe distance, one thing we have seen is the nest. This giant magpie built its nest in a location above the ground in a crater at the top of a mountain. (Usually, magpies build their nests in trees, but this is clearly really hard if you are bigger than a tree.) There are many ways to build a nest, including weaving, stitching, and stacking sticks. Instead of sticks, the giant magpie stacks together proportionally large trees, which maybe to the giant magpie LOOK like sticks.

Related Badge Skill:
AND THE
NEST IS
HISTORY

One of the coolest things about the giant magpie is how much it loves sparkly or shiny things, which it likes to place in its nest. (Did I mention that I also love shiny and sparkly things? I DO!) On the day Barney and I observed this giant magpie's nest, inside we found: a disco ball, three hubcaps, a toaster oven, a best-in-show trophy, a football, a surfboard, a blue kite, two grocery carts, a yellow bus, and a really large painting of a candy cane that was probably on top of a shopping mall at some point.

Since magpies build new nests every year, if the giant magpie is here to stay, we might want to nail down our appliances and other metal things next spring!

In the meantime, at a recent visit, Barney and I saw that, in addition to a snoozing giant magpie, the nest contained six pale white eggs! So we have provided below a few possible names for the future magpies of Miss Qiunzella Thiskwin Penniquiqul Thistle Crumpet's Camp for Hardcore Lady Types.

Moc Magpie
Doc Magpie
Keylime Magpie
3.14 Magpie
Lemon Meringue Magpie
Ted Magpie

(As a side note, did you know that the word PIE comes from the Latin word PICA, which means "magpie"? Pretty cool!)

Remember, a bird's nest is not for touching or interfering with in any way. To keep the baby birds and yourself safe, make sure you keep a respectful distance and don't touch the nest or eggs with your hands.

BEARWOMAN'S BREAKFAST SPECIAL

by RIPLEY (and KZYZZY)

CREATURE CATEGORY: Shape-Shifting Mammal

DANGER LEVEL: 5

HABITAT: Wherever she feels like being at any given time

DIET: See below

FAVORITE CATCHPHRASE: None of your business!

CREATURE PEEVES: Scouts, silliness, tomfoolery, scouts who are silly and foolish

There is probably no radder person at Miss Qiunzella's than Bearwoman.

It is hard to get to know Bearwoman because she doesn't really like talking to people. But here are a few awesome things about Bearwoman.

1. She's a shape-shifter who can be a bear or a person in a big giant coat with glasses.
2. She used to run the camp!
3. She used to run the camp when Rosie was a scout! How long ago was that? So long.
4. Her name is Nellie.

Research into different types of shape-shifters revealed the story of the Berserkers, Norse warriors who could change into wolves and bears as part of their battling skills. When asked if she was a Berserker, Bearwoman snarled and walked away.

For more information on shape-shifters, please see the section on the selkies (page 106) and Seafarin' Karen (page 94).

If you're ever wondering if the person you're looking at is Bear-woman, you can identify her by a few key features.

Her Coke-bottle-thick glasses

Her adorable crow's feet

Her tortoiseshell knee pads

Her coat of many furs

Because it was hard to get Bearwoman to sit down for an interview, I asked a few other people at camp about her.

MAL: When she talks, Bearwoman sounds like her voice comes from somewhere very old, a place that smells like the woods right after the rain.

MOLLY: Bearwoman is a master of vortexes (little slips of glimmer), at spotting them and traveling through them.

JO: Bearwoman is everywhere and nowhere.

APRIL: She acts like she's seen everything before and like she knew what was about to happen before it happened.

ROSIE: Nellie? She's a complex character.

Right after Rosie said that, she had to leave suddenly, wearing a set of metal crampons and a pair of thick metal gloves.

After I asked all those people, I was hungry, so I went to talk to Miss Qiunzella's master chef, Kzyzzy Koo. Who is also awesome. And she helped me with my research!

She told me that, on a specific day of the year, she wouldn't say which, Bearwoman eats the best breakfast in the world. Sort of. Kzyzzy calls it the Bearwoman Breakfast Special and Kzyzzy's daughter, Bun-Bun, takes it to Bearwoman at an unrevealed location at dawn.

So this is it!

BEARWOMAN BREAKFAST SPECIAL

On a wooden plate, which may also be a very flat piece of a tree, place:

> 3 cups blackberries
> 3 cups blueberries
> 3 cups raspberries
> 2 strawberries

Add a layer of grass (preferably pulled rather than cut). Dirt/clumps of earth are okay. On top of this layer add:

> 3 cups bees
> 3 cups grasshoppers
> $\frac{1}{2}$ cup wasps (stinger in)
> $2\frac{1}{2}$ cups ants (black)

Add an additional layer of corn, random roots, and leaves.

Finish with a generous sprinkling of grubs and beetle larvae and one very large fish (salmon preferred).

Serves 1.

No napkin or cutlery needed! Bearwoman likes to mash her own breakfast special to a pulp.

For scientific purposes, the members of Roanoke did consider trying Bearwoman's breakfast special. However, it was really difficult to find two cups of ants, so we decided to leave it.

KITTENS! KITTENS! KITTENS!

by RIPLEY

CREATURE CATEGORY: Mystical Feline

DANGER LEVEL: 3 (but varies greatly because cats are so unpredictable)

HABITAT: Laps, cozy spots on top of anything warm and/or recently washed

DIET: Cat food and cat treats

FAVORITE CATCHPHRASE: MEOW.

CREATURE PEEVES: Water, chills, empty food bowls

The following magical kittens were accidentally created by a wish by ME. They are all awesome. If I had another wish, I would create . . . MORE MAGICAL KITTENS!

Or, wait. Maybe I wouldn't.

OH YES I WOULD!

MARIGOLD

Description: Gold tabby mix
Powers: Can make herself as big as a really really big house. Or a really really big bus. Or a mountain!
Likes: Really really big balls of yarn and kitty back rides
Dislikes: Water

TATER TOTS

Description: Fire-orange-red tabby
Powers: Flame projection as well as full fur flame
Likes: Balls of tinfoil; just about the only cat toy he can't incinerate with a single FWOOOF of fire.
Dislikes: Water

CHESTER

Description: Soft fluffy white British shorthair
Power: Flight
Likes: Cat towers, trees, clouds
Dislikes: Water

TUGBOAT

Description: Chubby-wubby Bengal Maine coon mix
Powers: Floating, pop-out-of-nowhere abilities
Likes: Ear scratching, back scratching, little balls of fluff that float in the air
Dislikes: Water

JESSICA

Description: Brown with cute little orange ears and orange stripes and tail
Power: Sticks to actually anything, like a piece of Velcro but a cat
Likes: Carpets, curtains, and tapestries
Dislikes: Water

SCOOTS

Description: Orange with fluffy tail
Power: Walks through walls, caves, door. . . anything really
Likes: Walking through legs, purring really really loudly, string
Dislikes: Water

WRINKLEBUTT

Description: Hairless with puppy eyes
Power: Creates bubbles of protection around himself and whoever he's sitting on or cuddling with
Likes: Bubbles
Dislikes: Water

SPOT

Description: The most iguana-looking cat you ever saw, because she's an iguana who's also a cat
Power: Being an iguana
Likes: Bugs and grabbing things with her little paws
Dislikes: Water

I TON

PEANUT

Description: Black with smoky-gray spots
Power: Gravity pull (meaning that Peanut is the heaviest cat in the history of the world)
Likes: Being carried, laser dots on the wall
Dislikes: Water

PLOPSTOWN

Description: Chocolate brown with purple velvet scarf accessory
Power: Telekinesis, which means making people holding him and also other objects float and move
Likes: Slowly, gently, carefully scooting things off tables
Dislikes: Water

MR. CHIPS

Description: Tiger stripes and eyes and nose and maybe also a tiger
Power: Laser-light eyes (not to be confused with the lasers that cut through things)
Likes: Disco music, making other cats chase her lasers around
Dislikes: Water and mirrors

RODRIGUEZ

Description: Russian tabby mix with impossibly green eyes
Power: SONIC BOOM MEW
Likes: Butterflies, crawling up trees, mewing
Dislikes: Water

MR. JELLY

Description: Long-haired yellow cat
Power: Static SPARK
Likes: Sweaters, feather on a string
Dislikes: Water

BRUCE

Description: Black cat with ears like tea saucers
Power: Super hearing and a little bit of flight if he flaps his ears fast enough
Likes: Tuna, things that smell like tuna, cheek kisses
Dislikes: Water

PURR

DEBBIE

Description: Brown short hair with pointed tail
Power: Really good at snuggles
Likes: Batting at her reflection in the mirror
Dislikes: Water

SPIDEY

Description: Gray and white with eight legs
Power: Superfast kitty crawl and climb
Likes: Scratching posts
Dislikes: Water

SIMON

Description: Black cat with one red, one yellow, and one blue eye
Power: Floats
Likes: Curling up in a little ball in the middle of the room and purring
Dislikes: Water

SPOT THE SENTRY

by RIPLEY

CREATURE CATEGORY: Mystical Mineral

DANGER LEVEL: 7

HABITAT: Difficult to find

DIET: None

FAVORITE CATCHPHRASE: None

CREATURE PEEVES: None

The scouts of Roanoke first encountered the sentries when they were accidentally called to action by a mysterious voice. Fortunately, former scout Abigail, who is well versed in the ways of mystical creatures, saved the day and stopped the sentries from destroying the camp, which was also going through a time vortex issue at the time. This was a very complicated adventure, which involved various scouts getting very old or very young, and it was a solid reminder of the forces that lay in wait in the woods and wilderness.

Sentries are basically creatures that are always playing a game of hide-and-go-seek. Maybe they are the best hide-and-go-seek players in the universe, because they can stay very very still for a very long time. Sometimes even millennia.

I guess it's more like they're playing a really long game of wait then hurry up because they have to stay very very still until someone sends them a special signal calling them to protect something.

When they are protecting stuff, the sentries are almost unstoppable. Their footsteps shake the ground like little earthquakes. They can tear down forests like cobwebs.

This distinguishes sentry from stone guardians (see page 82), since stone guardians are always awake and ready for a fight.

But when are they are still, which is most of the time, they are like this really really cool secret in the woods.

See if you can spot the sentry!

CANOE SEE THE SENTRY
IN THIS PIC?

MAKING A SPLASH IN SENTRY FALLS!

SENTRY LOOKOUT WITH BARNEY AND JO!

JEN AND APRIL ON A SENTRY SPOTTING HIKE!

A FINAL WORD
FROM ROSIE

TO THE ESTEEMED MEMBERS OF THE BOARD OF SCOUTS

Hello, gals!

It's been one too many moons since our last cribbage marathon! I hope this letter finds you well. Sarah, thanks for the cookies. Cookie, thank you for the poultice. Polly, thank you for the enchanted lasso. It came in very handy this week, I can tell you (or you can just imagine).

Don't have a lot of time to write. As you know. Very busy. As usual!

Wanted to say I'm just so super-duper proud of these scouts. I think this is a pretty fascinating collection of very curious things. And as you know, very curious things are pretty much my thing.

So I hope you see your way to giving these scouts their BEAST. They deserve it. They did this all on their own. They put in the leg-work, the elbow grease, the whole kitten and caboodle! I've seen them everywhere, up mountains, in bogs and forests. They even checked in on what Nellie eats for breakfast! Can you imagine? Tried to interview her. Was quite a thing.

So. Yes. I hope you look kindly on this effort.

Have to go! Late night is a good time for tracking. The moon is up and I have adventure duties of my own.

Best,
R

LUMBER-JOY!!! WE DiD IT!

APPLICATION APPROVED!